LOVE UPO...

Verity had learned the words of Shakespeare by heart, but now her heart was pounding out of control as she had to give voice to them.

She was on a stage playing the part of Juliet before an avid throng and facing an irresistible Romeo in the form of the handsome, reckless, and rakish Brutus Ranley.

Trying to keep control of her sense and her senses was hard enough in public, but she faced an even greater challenge when the curtain came down.

For then a different drama would begin, created not by the Bard's quill but Cupid's quiver . . . a drama in which Ranley knew how to play his part all too well . . . a drama that made love upon the wicked stage seem like innocent child's play . . .

MARGARET SUMMERVILLE grew up in the Chicago area and holds degrees in journalism and library science. Employed as a librarian, she is single and lives in Morris, Illinois, with her Welsh corgi, Morgan.

The Improper Playwright

by

Margaret Summerville

A SIGNET BOOK

SIGNET
Published by the Penguin Group
Penguin Books USA Inc., 375 Hudson Street,
New York, New York, 10014, U.S.A.
Penguin Books Ltd, 27 Wrights Lane, London W8 5TZ, England
Penguin Books Australia Ltd, Ringwood, Victoria, Australia
Penguin Books Canada Ltd, 10 Alcorn Avenue, Toronto, Ontario, Canada M4V 3B2
Penguin Books (N.Z.) Ltd, 182-190 Wairau Road,
Auckland 10, New Zealand

Penguin Books Ltd, Registered Offices:
Harmondsworth, Middlesex, England

First published by Signet,
an imprint of New American Library, a division of Penguin Books USA Inc.

First Printing, March, 1992

10 9 8 7 6 5 4 3 2 1

 REGISTERED TRADEMARK—MARCA REGISTRADA

PRINTED IN THE UNITED STATES OF AMERICA

BOOKS ARE AVAILABLE AT QUANTITY DISCOUNTS WHEN USED TO PROMOTE
PRODUCTS OR SERVICES. FOR INFORMATION PLEASE WRITE TO PREMIUM
MARKETING DIVISION, PENGUIN BOOKS USA INC., 375 HUDSON STREET,
NEW YORK, NEW YORK 10014.

1

The Earl of Benbrook sometimes regretted that he had been overly indulgent with his daughter, Verity. The earl found himself thinking so as he sat at the breakfast table in the vast, drafty dining hall of Benbook Castle, looking across at his offspring. Verity had the stubborn, willful expression that oftentimes exasperated his lordship.

"You are not being reasonable, Verity," the earl said finally.

"Your father is right, Verity," said the Countess of Benbrook, who was also seated at the table. Lady Benbrook, an attractive woman of middle years, eyed her daughter with disapproval.

Verity stared down at her plate, and then looked over at her father. He seemed rather grim, but then his lordship was a serious gentleman, who seldom smiled. Gray-haired, tall, and dignified, the earl could be a formidable personage, but Verity was not in the least afraid of him. "Papa," she said, "you cannot expect me to be happy that you are tossing me out, forcing me to marry a man with whom I have no chance of happiness. Do you despise me so much that you can no longer bear my company?''

The last sentence was spoken with such melodramatic theatricality that Lord Benbrook had an uncharacteristic urge to burst into laughter. ''Good heavens, my girl, quit being ridiculous. You are two and twenty. You must marry and you must marry Dorchester.''

''And do cease acting as if Gerald were some sort of monster, Verity,'' said Lady Benbrook sternly. ''He is a very nice young man.''

''Yes, he is a good fellow,'' agreed the earl. ''Oh, I warrant he is a bit of a dudgeon, but you could do far worse. By my honor, you cannot put him off forever. You have been engaged for two years. There are many who consider Dorchester a very great prize. His father has of late been reminding me of that.''

Tears formed in Verity's eyes. ''How can you care so little for my feelings?''

''Damnation,'' muttered the earl. ''Verity de Lacy, you will not fool us with this playacting of yours. You may weep all you want, but we will not be swayed by crocodile tears.''

''Crocodile tears!'' Verity rose from the table. ''I do not know what I have done to receive such infamous treatment from my own father. I shall leave you to your breakfast. I am too miserable to eat.'' Pausing, she regarded her parents accusingly. ''I daresay you will not care if I starve myself to death!'' With these words, Verity made a dramatic exit from the dining room, causing the earl to mutter to himself before turning his attention to his kippers. The countess shook her head, as if wondering how she and her husband could have had such a wayward young lady for a daughter.

Verity was irritated and frustrated as she made her way through the meandering corridors of Benbrook Castle. Frowning, she walked up the stone staircase that led to her rooms. It was becoming increasingly difficult to waken the sympathies of her parents to her plight, she told herself. Tears and remonstrances were becoming quite ineffectual, for the earl and countess had hardened their hearts against their daughter's emotional displays.

By the time Verity arrived at her bedchamber, her tears and distraught expression had long vanished. Indeed, they had only been for her parents' benefit. As she entered the room, a thoughtful look appeared on Verity's countenance. She would have to change her strategy, she decided. She must devise some other way to postpone her wedding.

Verity de Lacy's reluctance to marry was a puzzlement to many, since her fiancé was greatly admired in the first circles. Gerald Hubert Mortimer, Marquess of Dorchester, was a young man of eminent lineage and enormous wealth. The heir to a dukedom, Dorchester had been the object of the dreams of numerous matchmaking society mamas.

The marquess was a solid and respectable gentleman, apparently immune to the vices that so often characterized men of his class and fortune. He kept no mistresses and he avoided gaming houses and spirits. He was also a very handsome man, tall and stately, with impressive manners.

Some, in truth, had difficulty finding fault with the marquess, although critical observers might say that he was something of a snob, a trifle self-important, and decidedly humorless. And although some might say as well that his lordship was a man of limited intellect, that was hardly considered a fault in aristocratic circles.

Verity had known the marquess since she had been a young girl. They had always gotten along well, despite differences in temperament, and Dorchester was fond of her.

For her part, although Verity did not dislike the marquess, she most certainly did not love him. This was to her a very great problem, for Verity was of a romantic nature and could not imagine marrying a man she did not adore.

Going to the window, Verity stood gazing out at the placid Lancashire countryside. From her second-story room, she had a marvelous view of the large park surrounding the castle. It was lovely that April morning with the grass glistening with dew and the newborn leaves looking green and fresh. Yet the beauty of the day was lost on Verity, who turned away from the window and sat down at the elegant cherry desk that graced one corner of the room.

Opening a drawer, she took out a pile of papers and perused them for a while. Then, taking up her pen and dipping it in ink, Verity began to write.

Anyone seeing Lady Verity de Lacy for the first time would have noted at once that she was a very pretty girl. Somewhat over average height, Verity had an excellent figure. Her oval countenance boasted good, regular features, and although the exacting standards of female beauty may have found some fault with her slightly turned-up nose and overgenerous lips, she was accounted a very attractive young lady by even the sternest of critics. Verity's large blue eyes were especially admired, blessed as they were with exotically thick black lashes. Her raven black hair was the envy of many of her acquaintances. It was arranged in ringlets about her face, creating a charming picture.

Engrossed in her writing, Verity was not thinking at all about her appearance. Indeed, she gave little attention to it, leaving such concerns as her hair and clothes to her diligent lady's maid, Nell Dawson.

That young woman soon made her appearance in Verity's room. Only a few years older than her mistress, Nell was plump and pleasant looking with blond hair and a smiling, dimpled countenance. "I heard you left the breakfast table, my lady. I've brought you some scones."

"You are a dear, Nell," said Verity. "I am famished."

The servant placed the plate of scones on the desk before her mistress. "I shall not disturb you, my lady. I see you are working."

"Do not go, Nell. I need your opinion."

"Yes, my lady?"

"I have killed off Sandor."

"Oh, my lady!" cried the servant. "Whyever did you do that?"

"I was vexed with him. But I do think it is a good idea."

She handed the pages of paper to Nell, who read them intently and then shook her head. "Poor Princess Thalia. It is really too sad, my lady."

"It is a tragedy, Nell. It is supposed to be sad. The entire audience should collapse into tears on hearing Thalia's last speech." Verity paused. "What do you think of Princess Thalia's killing herself with a dagger?"

"Oh, my lady!" cried Nell. "You would not do that!"

"I am not sure," replied Verity, taking the pages from her maid. "I do want to hear your opinion of that last speech."

"I did like it, my lady," returned Nell a bit hesitantly.

"Come, come, do not mince words, Nell."

"I do wonder about the last part, my lady. I do think your ladyship might reconsider the rhyme."

"Oh, that was troublesome," said Verity. "Perhaps you are right, Nell. I shall rework that."

That Lady Verity de Lacy was asking for editorial assistance from her maid, an untutored young woman of lowly origins, was quite remarkable. Yet, Nell was more to Verity than just a servant. She was a friend and confidante, the only person privy to Verity's secret. No one else had an inkling that Lady Verity wrote plays and fancied herself a playwright of some ability.

Her young ladyship's aspirations to become a playwright had begun in girlhood. When she was seven, Verity had accompanied her parents and brothers to the performance of a troupe of traveling players that had come to the village. While her brothers Walter and Edward had been unimpressed, Verity had been enthralled by the world of make-believe that had unfolded before her.

She soon began writing dramas, much to the disapproval of her governess, who preferred that her charge be more conscientious in doing her sums and learning her French verbs. By the time Verity had reached her teens, she had decided it would be best to keep her preoccupation with play-writing to herself. For several years she had concealed the fact that she was writing from everyone except loyal Nell.

Unknown to her parents, the library at Benbrook Castle was the secret storage place of more than two dozen plays written by the prolific authoress. There were comedies and tragedies, some of them dreadful and some remarkably good, but all of them lying unknown and unread.

"I do think *The Warrior Princess* is your ladyship's best play," said Nell. "Will you soon be finished with it?"

Verity nodded. "I should think so, Nell." She sighed. "And then I shall place it with all the others—to the oblivion of some dusty cupboard."

"That is dreadful, my lady," cried Nell. "You must not do so. It must be performed."

"Oh, Nell, don't be silly. That is impossible."

"I cannot understand why, my lady. It is monstrous good."

This remark brought a smile to Verity's face. "That is very kind of you, Nell. I know you like it and I do agree that it is my best work, but is it truly good enough for the theater? I daresay someone like Lord Ranley would scoff at it."

"He would not," said Nell firmly.

"Oh surely, Nell, you cannot think that the greatest playwright in all of England would not scorn my poor efforts."

"Indeed not, my lady," returned Nell stoutly. She paused and touched a finger to her lips in a thoughtful gesture. "I do say, my lady, that you have given me an idea. When you have finished *The Warrior Princess*, you must send it to Lord Ranley, asking for his opinion."

"Oh, Nell, that is ridiculous. I could not be so presumptuous as to ask Lord Ranley to read my poor effort." Verity shook her head, but Nell noted that her mistress seemed to be mulling the matter over. "Do you really believe he might do so—read the play and tell me what he thinks?"

"Indeed, he would, my lady. Your ladyship might at least try. Send it to him."

"But what if he hates it, Nell? What if he tells me that it is dreadful?"

"Then he is a poor judge of plays, my lady."

Verity laughed. "I fear you are not as harsh a critic as Lord Ranley doubtless is. But perhaps you are right. What harm will it do if I send it to him? The worst that will come of it is that he would tell me that I am hopelessly untalented and I should leave playwriting to those with an ounce of ability." Verity rose from her chair. "And then, my dear Nell," she continued in a theatrical voice, "I shall borrow Princess Thalia's dagger and end it all!"

"My lady!" cried the maid in horror, causing Verity to burst into gales of laughter.

2

John Charles Ranley, fifth Baron Ranley of Rotherfield, stood at a window in his sitting room, glumly surveying the London street outside his fashionable townhouse. After a time, he turned from the window and, sitting down at his cluttered desk, poured a glass of wine from a decanter.

"I beg your pardon, my lord," said a voice, and Ranley looked up to see a liveried footman enter the room. "Mr. Hawkins is here to see your lordship."

"Throw him out, Perkins," said the baron, downing his wine and then pouring another glass.

The servant nodded. "Yes, my lord."

Ranley watched the man vanish from the doorway. It was odd, he thought, that at times he found it strange to be addressed as "my lord." Although he had inherited the title two years ago, it still seemed peculiar to be a peer of the realm, the beneficiary of the privileges and courtesies bestowed upon a man of title.

Before the unexpected death of his uncle, the baron had been plain Mr. Ranley, playwright and actor, known to an adoring public as "Brutus" Ranley. The nickname had been given to him ten years ago when at the age of one and twenty he had first played Brutus in *Julius Caesar*. The role had been a great triumph, launching a splendid theatrical career which brought him fame and wealth. As time went on, Ranley had turned more to playwriting, producing numerous popular works, in many of which he took the lead.

Ranley had not expected to accede to the title of baron, for his uncle had been a vigorous gentleman, fifty years of age with a strong constitution and a new young wife. A riding accident had abruptly put an end to the fourth baron's life before his lady could provide him with an heir. And thus Brutus Ranley had become a man of rank and property.

There was, the baron knew, an irony in his inheriting the title, for his uncle had heartily disliked his nephew just as he had heartily disliked his younger brother, Ranley's father. Indeed, the brothers had not been on speaking terms since Ranley's father had scandalized the family by marrying an actress and going off to make his own way in the world. Ranley had never met his uncle, for that gentleman had steadfastly refused to receive him or communicate in any way with the son of his disgraced brother.

Becoming a lord had had advantages for Brutus Ranley. Although he had viewed with some cynicism the newfound respect accorded him due to his title, he had well appreciated the security a fine estate like Rotherfield had provided him. Since he now received a substantial income from the property, he could do exactly as he pleased.

Of course, being a peer of the realm had cut short Ranley's acting career, for a lord could hardly appear on stage. Although he had intended to continue writing plays, Ranley now seemed content to be a gentleman of leisure, idling his time away with gaming and drinking. This idleness quite dismayed Ranley's friend and associate, theater manager William Hawkins, who had counted on the baron's continued literary production. Yet Ranley's former prolific production of manuscripts had been cut drastically, and for months now he had hardly set pen to paper.

William Hawkins now stood at the doorway of Ranley's sitting room. His hands on his hips, Hawkins eyed the baron with disapproval. "Brutus, you scoundrel, how dare you refuse to see me!"

The baron frowned at his friend. "I asked my servant to toss you from my door, Billy. Apparently he did not succeed."

"Apparently not." Hawkins entered the room. He was a big, brawny, middle-aged man with graying hair and a serious expression on his face. Carefully dressed as a gentleman of means, Hawkins carried a silver-headed walking stick, which he swung back and forth as he glanced about the untidy room. He frowned at his friend's disheveled appearance.

Attired in a silk dressing gown, Ranley looked as though he had just risen from bed. His hair was tousled and his lean face was unshaven. Yet his present disorderly condition did not alter the fact that the baron was an exceptionally handsome man. His lordship's countenance was blessed with excellent classical features and the rather prominent chin of his Ranley ancestors that seemed to denote strong character. He had luminous brown eyes and dark hair that fell in waves over his wide, noble brow.

"Look at you, Brutus," said William Hawkins disgustedly. "I'm damned if you're not drunk. What is wrong with you?"

"If you carp at me, Billy, I shall toss you out myself."

"Toss me out?" scoffed the theater manager. "Try it, my lad, and you will see what Billy Hawkins is made of."

"I know what you are made of, Billy," replied Ranley wearily. "Now sit down and stop being disagreeable. Have some wine. Perkins will fetch you a glass. Perkins, a glass for Mr. Hawkins!" The baron's shout quickly brought his footman with the wine glass. "Now have a drink, Billy. It will settle your spleen."

Sitting down in an armchair near the baron, Hawkins ill-temperedly took the glass of wine that Ranley held out to him. "I will not beat about the bush, Brutus. I have come for the play."

"And what play is that, my dear William?" said the baron.

"Hang it, Brutus. You know very well I mean the play you promised me. I have been very patient with you, but I must have it and have it soon."

Ranley shrugged. "Then I fear I shall have to disappoint you. I have no play."

"You must have some of it. I shall take the first act."

Ranley rose unsteadily to his feet. "You don't understand, Billy. I don't have it. Not one act, not one page, not one word."

"You cannot be serious."

"I am quite serious. No, Billy, I have nothing for you."

Hawkins eyed the younger man in exasperation. "Then what am I to do? Everyone is clamoring for a new Ranley play."

"My dear friend, there are plays galore to be had, and better plays than I have ever written." Walking unevenly over to a sofa upholstered in striped silk, he plopped down on it. "Now I beg you, stop pestering me. I am very tired." The baron yawned and reclined on the couch. "Yes, do go away, Billy."

"I'll not go away until I say what should be said. You are ruining yourself, living as you do. Staying up all night, taking up with the worst reprobates, gaming, and drinking like a lord."

Ranley cast a sardonic look at the theater manager. "As well I should. I *am* a lord."

"Would to God you were not, for what good it's done you," muttered Hawkins. "You must take hold of yourself. For God's sake, Brutus, can you not see what you have become?"

This anquished question provoked no response from his

lordship, for Ranley, having closed his eyes and pillowed his head against the arm of the sofa, had fallen instantly to sleep. "Damnation!" cried Hawkins, rising from his chair and standing over the recumbent baron. "Wake up! I've not finished with you."

Ranley only mumbled something and passed deeper into an inebriated slumber. Hawkins folded his arms across his chest and shook his head. He was very fond of his young friend, despite his frustration with him at that moment. This made it more difficult to witness the baron's course of self-destruction.

Certainly, Brutus Ranley had always been a high-spirited young man. In his early days as an actor, he had been involved in a number of escapades that had resulted in his reputation as a hard-drinking ladies' man. Yet, throughout his theatrical career, Ranley had never missed a performance, nor appeared on stage in an intoxicated condition.

He had also written an astonishing number of plays, producing them with clocklike regularity. The Ranley plays as well as Ranley himself had been why Hawkins's Queen's Theater had achieved a success rivaling that of Drury Lane and Covent Garden.

It had, therefore, been a severe blow for Hawkins when Ranley inherited his title, for Hawkins had instantly lost his greatest actor and his theater's greatest asset. The theater manager had been very much relieved when Ranley had announced that he had no intention of abandoning his playwriting despite the fact that scribbling plays was hardly the proper occupation for a baron. Things had gone well at first, but then a year ago, Ranley's last play was savagely ridiculed by a critic in the *Morning Chronicle*.

What would not have bothered the old Brutus Ranley now seemed unbearably irksome to Lord Ranley of Rotherfield. He seemed to lose interest in his plays and in the theater in general. Taking up the life of a gentleman of fashion, Ranley had plunged with a vengeance into the world of the sporting gentleman. He had also given up most of his theatrical friends, apparently preferring his new, more aristocratic acquaintances.

As he continued to gaze down at Ranley, Hawkins felt an acute sense of disappointment. He had been relying on the baron for a new play, for Ranley had promised very solemnly some months ago that he would have it completed. Yet the baron had been putting him off for weeks, claiming that the muse had temporarily flown or something of that nature.

Turning away from his sleeping friend, Hawkins glanced around the sitting room once more. Ranley's desk was piled with papers strewn about in disorderly fashion. "He must have been writing something," said Hawkins to himself. "Perhaps it is somewhere amidst this rubble." Deciding to investigate, the theater manager sat down at the desk and began to look through the mess.

He found numerous letters, including several billets-doux from lovelorn ladies. After reading these with great interest, Hawkins tossed them aside. He then sifted through tradesman's bills and invitations, finding no evidence of Ranley's work, save for a few scraps of unfinished poetry.

"But what is this?" Hawkins said aloud as his eyes fell upon a stack of papers on the corner of his desk. Eagerly grasping the pages, the theater manager flipped through them. He was pleased to see that it was a play. "Thank God," exclaimed Hawkins. "The rogue did write something."

The play was neatly copied in a meticulous rounded hand. Its title page said, *The Warrior Princess—A Tragedy*. Hawkins read the first page and then the next, thinking that the drama was off to a promising start. He continued reading, and when he was done, he pulled a handkerchief from his pocket and wiped a tear from his eye. It was a wonderful play, filled with the sort of conflict and pathos his audience loved. He knew it would be a great success.

Looking over at Ranley, who was still sleeping soundly, Hawkins wondered why the baron had not given him the play. It was very peculiar, he thought. Then out of the corner of his eye, he caught sight of a letter. "My lord," it began. "I should be most grateful if you would read my play, *The Warrior Princess.*"

"Damnation!" cried Hawkins, perusing the letter. It was signed by a V. de Lacy, of Lancashire. So it was not Ranley's play, Hawkins told himself, but the work of some would-be playwright from the north country. What a very great pity, decided the theater manager. Had it been Ranley's work, it would have been very valuable indeed, but as the work of an unknown, it was considerably less so.

Ranley had a tremendous following and now that his numerous admirers could not see him act upon the stage, they wanted to see his plays. Why, at several recent performances the audiences had become quite unruly, shouting that they wished to see a new play, a new Ranley play. Hawkins had had to speak to them, assuring them that Baron Ranley was hard at work on a new work that would be ready very soon. Hawkins shook his head. If only this play had been the baron's.

The theater manager sat for a time thinking. The light of an idea came to his eyes as he reread the title page of *The Warrior Princess.* This may not be Ranley's play, but who would know that? It could be changed a bit here and there and no one would be the wiser. And who was this V. de Lacy anyway, but a nobody from the provinces? Why, if the title were changed, who would ever know it was not Ranley's work?

All he would have to do would be have the play copied with a few revisions made here and there. Hawkins grinned. He would have his new Ranley play and everyone would be delighted. Glancing at the sleeping baron, Hawkins's grin vanished briefly. What would Brutus say? He would not be at all happy. Hawkins shrugged and smiled again. He really did not care what Ranley would think or do. Indeed, why be concerned about that when the baron was going about in a fog most of the time anyway.

After rummaging about in Ranley's desk drawers, Hawkins produced a piece of paper. He began to write. "Dear Mr. de Lacy, I have read your play. I regret that I find it . . ." Hawkins paused and then continued, "without merit of any kind. I strongly suggest you give up playwriting, sir. To be blunt, your abilities obviously do not lie in this direction. Your Servant, Ranley."

Apparently well satisfied with this missive, Hawkins blotted it and then folded it. With one last look at Ranley's recumbent form, he picked up the manuscript and departed.

3

The Countess of Benbrook was growing increasingly bored with life at Benbrook Castle. Her ladyship had never liked the castle, for it was a gloomy, uncomfortable residence set on the heather moorlands of southern Lancashire. The countess was very eager to go to London where she would rush headlong into the excitement of the London Season with its balls and parties and gossip.

As she sat in the drawing room staring absently at a novel, Lady Benbrook reflected that it was unfortunate that she was the only member of her family anxious to leave for town. The earl preferred the country, and although Verity loved London, this year she seemed perfectly content to stay in Lancashire. This, her ladyship knew, was due to Verity's reluctance to face Dorchester and his family.

The countess frowned as she thought of her daughter's unfortunate reluctance to marry. Verity had always been the most difficult of her children. The two boys were no trouble in the least, but then they were still very young and they were away at Eton most of the time.

Verity had always been so stubborn and so subject to flights of fancy. And for some unaccountable reason, she had taken such a strong dislike to the idea of marrying Dorchester. Lady Benbrook sighed and turned her attention to the book in her lap.

She was soon interrupted by the appearance of her head-strong daughter. "I do not mean to bother you, Mama."

"My dear girl, you are not bothering me. Indeed, I am quite bored and am glad of company. Do sit down."

As Verity sat beside her mother on the sofa, Lady Benbrook reflected that her daughter looked very lovely in her new morning dress of pale blue jaconet muslin.

"What are you reading, Mama?"

"Oh, it is that book by Mrs. Radcliffe. I have never finished it." Verity suppressed a smile. Her mother had been attempting to read this book for more than a year, but it seemed she never got beyond the first few chapters. "And how have you been spending your morning, Verity? You have been secreted away in your room. I fear you spend too much time there by yourself, my dear. I will be so glad when we go to London. There will be so much to amuse you there."

Verity acknowledged this comment with a nod. Her mother's mention of London made her think of the play she had sent to Lord Ranley more than three weeks ago. She had had no reply, and although she knew that not very much time had passed, it was difficult to keep from worrying. What if Ranley hated the play or what if he did not reply at all?

Lady Benbrook noted her daughter's preoccupation. "Is something wrong, my dear?"

"Oh, no, Mama, nothing is wrong."

"I do not know why your father insists on staying in Lancashire for so long. The Season has started. Everyone is in town. And, of course, Dorchester is there."

"Oh, Mama," cried Verity, "why must you mention his name?"

"Good heavens, my dear, he is the man you are to marry. I daresay I shall mention his name upon occasion."

"I pray you change the subject, Mama, or we are bound to quarrel."

"You know there is no one who detests quarreling more than I do, Verity, but one must talk of these things. You know that we will be going to town very soon. You will see Dorchester and you will be agreeable. And we must set a date for your wedding. Do not protest. We all must marry, my dear. It is a lady's fate."

"I should be happier if I never married."

"Verity!" cried her mother in horror. "Never married? One must marry. Why, how else could one move about in Society?"

"I do not care a fig for Society," said Verity stubbornly.

"You are speaking nonsense," returned the countess. "And although I will not deny that many find husbands rather bothersome, they can be most convenient creatures, especially if they are wealthy. And Gerald is as rich as Croesus, and he is no lickpenny to be sure. You will be a very great lady, one day a duchess."

"Oh, Mama, why can't you understand? I do not love Gerald. I could never marry unless I was truly in love."

The countess shook her head. "Verity," she said severely, "it is time you threw off these childish fancies. I do not mean that it would not be a very good thing to marry a man one loved, but it is seldom practical. You will love Gerald in time."

Verity was about to protest that she would never love Gerald, but she was prevented from doing so by the appearance of a footman. "The post," said Lady Benbrook, happy for the diversion. "I do hope there are letters from town. I am starved for news."

The footman approached and extended a silver salver toward his mistress, who took several lettes from it. "Oh, here is a letter from Lady Cowper. She always has the best gossip. And here is a letter for you, Verity. I do not recognize the hand. It must not be from Gerald. He is not a very faithful correspondent, I must say.''

Since she had been awaiting a reply from Ranley, Verity viewed the arrival of letters with a mixture of anticipation and dread. Taking the missive from her mother, she eagerly broke the seal and opened it. Her eye immediately flew to the signature at the end of the short messsage. Ranley! He had replied!

A tremor of excitement passed through her as she began to read. Racing over the words, her expression changed quickly to a look of despair. The phrases ''without merit of any kind'' and ''abilities obviously do not lie in this direction'' hit her like blows. ''I strongly advise you to give up playwrighting.'' Verity read the sentence over and over. It could not be true! The foremost playwright in England was telling her to abandon what she loved most in all the world.

Lady Benbrook was so eager to read her letter that she did not concern herself much with Verity. When she did look up, she was startled to see that daughter's distraught look. ''Verity, what is the matter?''

''The matter?'' Verity tried to compose herself. ''Nothing is the matter, Mama.''

''You looked quite upset, as if you had disturbing news. Who is the letter from?''

''Oh, it is nothing of consequence. Just a note from Carolyn Billingham.''

''Poor Carolyn,'' said the countess. ''Such a very plain girl. How lucky for her that she will have such a generous marriage portion. I do hope she is well.''

''Oh, yes, Mama.'' Verity rose from the sofa. ''Do excuse me, Mama. I should write to Carolyn.''

''Surely that could be put off for a time, my dear.''

''I should like to do it at once. It will not take long.'' Verity did not wait for her mother to say anything else, but hurried from the room. Although the countess thought her daughter's abrupt departure rather peculiar, she only shrugged and returned to Lady Cowper's letter.

When Verity arrived in her bedchamber, she threw herself down upon her bed and burst into tears. Ranley had hated her play! How could she go on living?

Nell Dawson, who had been tidying things in her mistress's dressing room, heard Verity's sobs and hurried in. "My lady! Whatever is the matter?"

"Oh, Nell," Verity managed to say, still clutching the letter in her hand. She thrust it toward her maid. "See what he has said! He hated the play!"

"Oh, my lady!" Nell took the rather crumpled paper from her mistress and read it. "You must not allow this to discourage you, my lady."

"Not discourage me! Nell, you are as much a goose as I am! If Lord Ranley judges me as a terrible playwright, I am indeed that."

"Perhaps he is not so clever as they say," said Nell. " 'Tis a very rude letter by my way of thinking. Why, he might have said why he did not like it."

"He is a busy man, Nell," said Verity, sitting up on the bed and taking the letter from her maid. "He cannot be expected to waste time on such things. Oh, if only I had not sent him the play. How he must have laughed."

"Then he is a rude man," said Nell. "Your ladyship should not take what he says to heart."

"How could I not take it to heart? Oh, Nell, my life is over!"

"You cannot mean that, my lady."

"But I do mean it, Nell." Rising from the bed, Verity wiped her eyes with her handkerchief. "I shall never be happy again. Were I an ancient Roman, I should throw myself upon my sword."

"Lady Verity!"

"Yes, I would indeed." Verity placed her hand over her

eyes in what she hoped was a convincing gesture of despair. She sighed. "But this is not that antique age, Nell, so I shall be forced to live on and on in misery."

"Come, come, my lady, 'tis not so bad as that."

"It is as bad as that, Nell. Now, I beg you. Leave me."

Nell nodded. "Very well, my lady, but I shall be nearby. You must call if you need me." The maid made a quick curtsy and departed, leaving Verity to pace across the room in some agitation.

Although she had often considered that fact that Ranley might not like her play, Verity had not actually believed that he would hate it. She had been so proud of it, thinking it her greatest achievement. Whatever would she do now that her dreams were shattered?

Walking over to the window, she looked out. Yes, life would go on. She would be like everyone else. She would go to parties and balls and speak nonsense and pretend to enjoy herself. And she would marry Gerald and live a life of joyless tedium.

Verity stood in her room for a long time. Then, apparently growing restless, she left it. Descending the winding stone staircase, she made her way to the drawing room where her mother was still sitting.

"Verity?" said the countess. "Are you ill?"

"No, Mama," said Verity, managing a smile. "I have been thinking about things, Mama. I have reached a decision."

"A decision?"

Verity nodded. "I have been foolish not wishing to marry Gerald. I daresay you and Papa are right to be vexed with me. I shall give you no further trouble on that subject. Indeed, I have decided that I shall marry Gerald as soon as everything can be arranged."

"Oh, Verity," cried Lady Benbrook, rising to her feet. "This is wonderful news. Whatever has changed your mind?"

"It is just that I gave the matter very serious consideration.

I know that you are right. I have been ridiculous. I do think we should tell Papa that it is time we left for London. Why, the Season is going on without us.''

"Yes, that is what I have been saying for some weeks. Now that you have reached this excellent decision, I am sure your father will be as eager to go to town as I am. Oh, Verity, I am so happy!''

The countess joyfully embraced her daughter and Verity did her best to fight back tears.

4

It was past noon when Lord Ranley rose and wearily suffered the ministrations of his valet. The servant, who was well accustomed to his master's moods, knew at once that the baron was in a melancholy state that day. Indeed, his lordship often appeared so after a long night of gaming and drinking.

The valet, whose name was Tucker, prudently adjusted his mood to match his master's. He appeared solemn and said little as he went about his work. By the time he assisted the baron into his flawlessly cut coat of olive superfine, Ranley's seemed somewhat more cheerful. His lordship glanced briefly into the mirror, happy to see that despite the fact that his eyes were somewhat bloodshot and his complexion rather sallow, he looked quite presentable.

Ranley always cut a very fine figure. Although he had little patience with the dandy's obsession with fashion, he was careful to dress well. He patronized London's finest tailors, who thought it a very great honor indeed to have the famous Brutus Ranley as a customer.

Leaving his room, the baron went downstairs. There he settled himself in the drawing room to examine his mail and the newspapers, and then he ordered luncheon. After consuming an excellent meal and drinking only one glass of wine, Ranley found that his mood had changed completely and that he was now in unusually good spirits. Deciding to go out, he called for his carriage.

The coachman was a bit surprised to see his lordship venturing out so early in the day. Throughout the past months he had gone out only at night, usually returning in the early morning hours. The coachman was even more surprised to hear his master's instructions. "To the Queen's Theater, Burke."

"Aye, my lord," said the servant, maneuvering the baron's high-stepping bay horses into the street.

Ranley allowed a slight smile to cross his lips. He was sure that Burke, the coachman, must think it odd that he was going to the theater, for he had not been there in ages. In fact, the baron himself thought it very peculiar that the desire to see the old place had come to him so firmly that afternoon.

As the horses made their way down the street, Ranley looked out at the passing scenery. There were row upon row of fashionable townhouses interspersed with green parks. There were primroses blooming here and there and birds singing in trees. It occurred to Ranley that he seldom noticed such things any more.

He was only vaguely aware that pedestrians on the street recognized him as he went by, nudging their companions to point out the famous Lord Ranley. The baron cared little for celebrity now, although there had been a time not so very long ago when he had gloried in the acclaim of the multitude. The thought that his fame was passing did not in the least dismay him.

When the phaeton arrived at the Queen's Theater, Ranley regarded the familiar structure with an affectionate gaze. It had been the scene of so many of his triumphs and disasters. He thought of the theater like an old mistress he had abandoned, and it was with a feeling akin to guilt that he now approached it.

The Queen's Theater was one of the great dramatic centers of London. It had first been built in Queen Anne's time, hence the name. The building now standing was the third Queen's Theater for the two others before it had burned in equally disastrous fires. Bigger and grander than its predecessors and designed in the neoclassical style, it had the look of a Greek temple. Inside, it boasted five tiers of boxes, a gallery, a pit and a stage large enough for the most magnificent productions.

As Ranley jumped down from the carriage and walked toward the entrance, he thought of the day he had first entered this august shrine to the dramatic arts. He had just turned twenty-one and he was to play his first major role on a London stage. His Brutus was an overwhelming success, followed by many other memorable roles. Ranley had brought his audiences to their feet time and time again.

"Why 'tis Milord Brutus!" cried a voice as the baron entered the theater.

"Jenkins, you varlet," returned Ranley, grinning at an elderly man dressed in a drab coat. Jenkins had once been an actor, but now worked at the theater. In what capacity, Ranley did not know.

"How good it is to see you, my lord."

The baron shook the old man's hand. "You're looking well, Jenkins."

"Kind of you to say so, my lord. They are rehearsing your new play. I expect that is why you have come."

"My new play, Jenkins?" He regarded the old man in some surprise.

"Aye, *Valiant Lady,* and if I may say so, 'tis your lordship's finest work. So stirring and such pathos! And Mrs. Fleming is magnificent."

"So you think it my best work? How good of you," said Ranley. "Where is Hawkins? I think I should have a word with him."

"Mr. Hawkins is at the rehearsal. Go ahead, sir. He will be very glad to see you."

"Yes, I'm certain of that, Jenkins." The baron left the old man and proceeded into the theater where he found the company of actors engaged in dress rehearsal. They were wearing costumes that looked like those of ancient Greece or Rome. Mrs. Fleming, the *grande dame* of the Queen's Theater, was standing center stage attired in glittering finery. Her low-cut costume accentuated her voluptuous figure. She gestured broadly and spoke her lines with thunderous clarity.

Spotting Hawkins seated in the audience, Ranley joined him. The theater manager looked startled as his friend appeared and sat down in the seat next to him. "Ranley! What the devil are you doing here?"

"I have come to see my new play, Billy. Odd, but I seem to have forgotten writing it."

"Oh, your pardon, Brutus, but I must see this part. It has been causing some difficulty."

After directing a sidelong glance at Hawkins, Ranley then turned his attention to the stage. Mrs. Fleming was speaking again, her stentorian tones filling the empty theater. A handsome young man raced toward her and shouted something about an invasion. This caused general pandemonium on the stage, with all the male members of the cast waving swords or spears and affecting bellicose postures. Mrs. Fleming raised her lovely face toward the heavens and the curtain fell.

"Excellent," murmured Hawkins. "This is wonderful. That is the end of act two. Yes, yes, it is going very well indeed. It is a wonderful play."

"I am sure of that," said Ranley dryly. "But, old friend, I do wish you would remind me when I wrote it."

"I suppose I should explain," said Hawkins. "Yes, it is really quite easy to do so." The theater manager had given some thought to what he would say to Ranley when that gentleman heard about the play. He paused, wondering which explanation he should attempt. "You know very well you

did not write this, Brutus. That is, you did not write it
exactly."

Ranley's dark eyebrows arched slightly. "I did not write
it exactly?"

"No, but it is your play."

"And why is that, Billy?"

"Good God, Brutus, surely you remember that day some
three weeks ago when I came for the play."

"I have some recollection of it," returned the baron. In
truth, his memory of the occasion was hazy. He seemed to
recall Hawkins haranguing him about his failure to have
produced a play. He had been roaring drunk, he knew.

"I was very vexed with you, my dear lad, for you had
not one word written down. But then as we talked, you said
you had an idea for a play."

"I did?"

Hawkins nodded. "You were in your cups, of course, but
the words came pouring out. I took everything down as you
spoke. It was a wonderful story. Of course, I did fill in much
of the dialogue, but it is your play. You must remember some
of what you said."

"I do not have the least notion what you are talking about,"
said the baron uncertainly. He wondered if Hawkins was
quizzing him. Could he have come up with a story for a play
and then have completely forgotten it? It seemed quite
impossible, but then one's mind could certainly do strange
things when under the influence of spirits.

"It is the truth, my dear boy. Oh, I know I should have
called upon you to tell you, but I have been so busy. We
have had so little time. This will be a very great success,
I assure you. You must stay and watch act three."

"I should not miss it," replied Ranley.

"And Mrs. Fleming is so pleased with her part. Yes, yes,
it is an excellent play. I am sure you will remember some
of it as you see the third act."

The baron looked over at his friend once again. Hawkins
appeared quite serious, but he was a rogue at heart and one

could never really trust him. Ranley had a very strange
feeling as the third act began. Was it familiar or wasn't it?
Could he remember anything at all about this fantastic story
that was unfolding before him?

Ranley continued watching, hoping that something would
jog his memory. If he had come up with this story, thought
the baron, he must have been sleepwalking or delirious. It
was not a bad play. On the contrary, it was quite good with
intelligent dialogue and plentiful action. Mrs. Fleming was
relishing her part, playing it so broadly as to be almost comic.
Having spied Ranley in the audience, Mrs. Fleming seemed
to direct her lines to the baron, winking and batting her
eyelashes at him at every opportunity.

Ranley acknowledged her with a nod. Seven years ago,
he and the famed Maria Fleming had had an affair that had
set tongues wagging throughout London. It had lasted but
a few short, strenuous months and then had ended abruptly
when Maria had taken up with a Russian prince. Strangely
enough, Ranley had experienced only minor annoyance at
Mrs. Fleming's infamous conduct, and the two of them had
remained on friendly terms.

When the rehearsal was over, the cast members hurried
to greet Ranley. Since many of them were old friends and
colleagues, the baron was very pleased to see them. Shaking
hands with everyone, he smiled affably.

Mrs. Fleming had vanished, but she soon reappeared. The
others parted for her, allowing her to approach her old
paramour. "My dear Brutus!" cried the actress, kissing
Ranley on the cheek. "I thought you would never come to
see us. Do you not think that we have done justice to your
play?"

"You were wonderful. You were all wonderful."

Maria Fleming smiled brightly and Ranley found himself
thinking that she looked splendid dressed in her flowing
Grecian costume. She was certainly a handsome woman.
Nearly forty, Mrs. Fleming was still a great beauty with
marvelous red hair and buxom figure.

"Why have you stayed away from us so long, Brutus?" said Maria. "How bad of you, my dear, to abandon us."

"Indeed so," said Billy Hawkins. "But you will stay with us today. The play opens tonight. And afterward we will have a celebration of our triumph."

Ranley smiled. "I should like nothing better than a celebration."

"Good," returned Hawkins, clapping his friend on the back. As the others engaged the baron in conversation, Hawkins smiled with relief and marveled at how easy it was to hoodwink such a clever fellow as Brutus Ranley.

5

Although the Earl of Benbrook never looked forward to spending time in London, he was not at all reluctant to set out for town after hearing of Verity's change of heart. Scarcely believing his good fortune that his daughter was acting rationally, the earl had decided that they had best hurry to London before Verity changed her mind. There had then been a rush of activity as maids and footmen hurried about getting everything in readiness for the journey.

Lady Benbrook did not fail to note that her daughter seemed uncharacteristically melancholy during the preparation for the journey to town. Yet her ladyship was so pleased that Verity was finally showing some common sense that she did not give much thought to her daughter's apparent unhappiness. After all, reasoned Lady Benbrook, Verity would get over it in time. Indeed, soon they would be all so caught up in the excitement of the London Season that Verity would forget about her silly reluctance to marry Gerald.

The earl's traveling coach was soon packed and readied.

A commodious vehicle that could comfortably seat six inside, the carriage was very grand. As it passed through the numerous villages on the way to London, many heads were turned to see the splendid coach with the earl's coat of arms emblazoned on its doors.

Inside were Lord and Lady Benbrook, Verity, Nell, and the countess's maid Antoinette, a talkative French woman who chattered on at the least encouragement from anyone. Also in the carriage was Lady Benbrook's little dog, Jackanapes, who slept contentedly on his mistress's lap.

The journey from Benbrook Castle to London took nearly four days. After being jostled for so long on the highway, and spending three nights in inns, Lord and Lady Benbrook were very pleased when the coach finally arrived in town.

Verity, however, expressed no happiness as they made their way through the familiar busy streets. Usually she was filled with eager anticipation at finding herself in the great metropolis, but now she appeared glum and indifferent. She realized that she had not been the best of traveling companions on the way, for throughout most of the long ride, she had said very little, only making polite replies to questions. Yet how could she be cheerful when the dismal fate of marrying Lord Dorchester awaited her in town?

Even the idea of attending the London theater, long Verity's great love, seemed to hold no attraction for her. How could she bear to see the work of other playwrights, knowing that she herself could never join their ranks? No, life in town held no joys for Verity, and she gazed out the carriage window in glum silence.

Nell Dawson was frankly worried about her mistress, for she had never seen that young lady so dispirited. When they had started on the journey, Nell had expected that Verity would come around in a day or two. Her young ladyship always loved traveling and usually entertained everyone else with amusing tales and commentary about what they saw along the road.

Nell sincerely hoped that Verity would soon recover from

the disappointment she had experienced. It seemed abominable to Nell that a gentleman like Lord Ranley would inflict such harm with his careless letter. To say that Lady Verity had no ability was outrageous, thought Nell. Why, her mistress was the most talented young woman in the kingdom. The very thought of Baron Ranley infuriated Nell, and she vowed that should she ever see that gentleman, lord or no, he would get a well deserved tongue lashing.

The Earl of Benbrook owned a magnificent residence in one of the most exclusive areas of the city. Benbrook House, as it was called, was of recent construction and the Prince Regent himself had pronounced it one of the finest structures to grace London. As the carriage pulled up in front of the stately, elegant house, the earl was filled with justifiable pride. Living at Benbrook House, he thought, was the one consolation of being in London and putting up with the constant turmoil of society affairs.

While the countess could hardly contain her joy as she was assisted from the carriage by a footman, her daughter still appeared disheartened. Verity allowed herself to be assisted down from the coach, and as she walked toward the door of Benbrook House, she felt miserable. If only she could have stayed in Lancashire, she thought glumly. Now she would have to go out among Society and pretend to be cheerful. Fighting back a sudden urge to burst into tears, Verity followed her mother into the house.

Feeling somewhat better after a good night's sleep, Verity was relatively cheerful when Nell entered her room to assist her to dress. When she joined the earl and countess for breakfast, Verity appeared far less gloomy and Lady Benbrook was very much encouraged.

After breakfast Verity and the countess went to the linen drapers and Verity tried to express the appropriate amount of interest in the silks and satins presented by the efficient clerk. After making a number of purchases, the countess and her daughter returned home where they had a pleasant luncheon.

Later that afternoon, callers began to arrive at Benbrook House. Casting quick glances at the cards presented to her by the butler, the countess dismissed the visitors with a wave of her hand. "We are not receiving, Weeks."

"I cannot imagine how everyone knows we have arrived so quickly," said Verity.

"You know how news flies about. I daresay many saw the carriage."

"It can hardly be missed," said Verity nodding. "I am so glad we are not receiving, Mama."

"But my dear, we are not 'not receiving.' It is just that no one has arrived whom I would wish to see. I should certainly receive any of my dear friends. Ah, here is Weeks again. Who is it this time?"

The butler bowed and presented the salver, upon which was a calling card. "The Duchess of Haverford and Lord Dorchester, my lady."

"Gerald and his mother!" cried Verity. "Oh, I do not wish to see them."

"Now, my dear, we can hardly refuse to admit them."

Verity started to protest, but stopped. "Very well, Mama. I suppose there is little point in trying to avoid Gerald."

"That is very good of you, Verity." The countess turned to the butler. "Do show her grace and Lord Dorchester in to us."

Weeks nodded and left, returning shortly with the visitors. "Her grace, the Duchess of Haverford, and Lord Dorchester," he intoned solemnly.

"My dear Kate," said Lady Benbrook, rising to her feet and going to meet the duchess, whom she embraced and kissed on the cheek. "And dear Gerald. How handsome you look."

Verity had risen also and greeted the duchess with a curtsy. "My dearest Verity," cried the duchess enfolding the young lady to her ample bosom.

Lord Dorchester bowed politely over Lady Benbrook's hand and then turned to Verity. "You cannot know how glad I am to see you, Verity."

"That is very good of you, Gerald," replied Verity.

"Do sit down, my dears," said the countess. "How I have longed to see you both. I do hope the duke is well."

"Tolerable well, ma'am," said Dorchester, waiting until the ladies were seated and then sitting down on the sofa beside Verity.

"His gout has been plaguing him a little, I fear," said the duchess. As her grace filled them in on the duke's medical problems, Verity found herself studying first the duchess and then her future husband. Catherine, Duchess of Haverford, was a pale, stout woman of approximately fifty years of age. Her bearing was aristocratic and her expression usually solemn, giving her an imposing and rather forbidding look. She was splendidly dressed in a pelisse of gray kerseymere trimmed with velvet. On her head was a bonnet of ruby velvet decorated with lace and a plume of ostrich feathers.

Gerald Mortimer, Lord Dorchester, was also an imposing personage. Twenty-six years of age, he was very tall and magnificently attired. Verity noted that Gerald, who took keen interest in fashion, looked the part of the stylish dandy. He wore a tight-fitting coat over a mustard-colored waistcoat adorned with a number of gold fobs. His snowy white neckcloth was intricately tied and his nankeen pantaloons and gleaming Hessian boots fit his slim legs snugly.

Dorchester was undeniably handsome with lean, aristocratic features and abundant sandy-colored hair. His appearance was marred only by his humorless expression, for he rarely smiled and the corners of his mouth were fixed into a permanent frown.

"We are so happy that you have finally arrived in town," said the duchess. "Gerald was beside himself wishing you were here, Verity."

This remark caused Verity to suppress a smile, because she could not imagine Dorchester ever being "beside

himself'' over anything. He appeared a trifle embarrassed
by the remark. "I am glad to see you, Verity," he said. "I
do hope you had a pleasant journey."

"It was a very long journey, Gerald, but pleasantly
uneventful."

"Indeed," said the countess. "We did stay in a most
unpleasant inn. If you would have but seen what they called
boiled beef there."

"Oh, there are so many trials in traveling about," said
the duchess. "I am glad the duke's principal seat is so close
to town. And staying in public inns is the most frightful
experience!"

"Indeed so," said Dorchester. "One should avoid doing
so if at all possible. I cannot think when I last stayed at such
an establishment. Oh, yes, it was that dreadful trip to the
continent. My dear ladies, if one thinks our English inns are
not up to the mark, one must but spend a night in a French
establishment. I shudder at the thought."

Verity eyed her fiancé with disapproval. She loved
traveling and she enjoyed staying at inns. Adventuresome
by nature, Verity thought it well worth facing bedbugs and
unpalatable food in order to see the world. How she would
love to go to France, she thought, frowning at the marquess.

Verity was glad that the duchess changed the subject,
chattering on about a number of friends and relatives as well
as the general gossip about the Prince Regent and his family.
Verity, usually interested in the goings-on in the city, barely
listened to the conversation. She was once again plunged into
gloomy reflection.

Her mother's words shook Verity from her revery. "My
dear, don't you think it is good of Gerald to invite us to the
theater?"

"The theater?" said Verity, looking at the countess in
confusion. "Oh, yes, to be sure."

"I know how much you love it," said Dorchester.
"Heaven knows why. I have never had any liking for play-
actors strutting about making preposterous speeches. I find

it so dull." He managed a slight smile. "But everyone is talking about this play. And indeed, there is no point in having a box at the theater if one is never going to use it."

"I daresay it will be fun," said the duchess. "Mrs. Fleming is very good, they say. Do you know she has cast off Lord Greyson for Sir Arthur Cavendish? But then Sir Arthur does have twenty thousand a year."

"I find the woman frightfully vulgar," sniffed Dorchester. "But then, all actresses are so common. I should be perfectly happy if I never attended the theater, but . . ." The marquess looked indulgently at Verity. "I shall tolerate it for your sake."

"How kind of you, Gerald," said Lady Benbrook. "What a considerate young man you are. You see what a fortunate girl you are, Verity."

"Indeed I do," said Verity with some irony.

"It is I who am fortunate," said the marquess generously. "I do look forward to our theater engagement tomorrow evening."

"Yes, it will be quite lovely," said the duchess. "But, my dear Jane, you must excuse us. I promised I would call on Lady Jersey this afternoon." The guests made their farewells, leaving Verity and her mother.

Lady Benbrook seemed well pleased by the visit. "Gerald looked very handsome, did he not, Verity?"

"Yes, very handsome," said Verity.

"And he is so fond of you. Why, to take us to the theater when he so detests it. That is good of him. You see, he will be an indulgent husband—I am sure of it."

"Gerald indulgent? I hardly think so, Mama. Do not believe that he will keep attending the theater for my sake after we are married."

"Verity!"

"Oh, Mama, you know him better than that. But do not worry. It does not signify in the least if I never go to the theater. Indeed, I should prefer not to go. I should have told Gerald that there is no need to subject himself to an evening of intolerable boredom on my account. No, Mama, I do not wish to go to the theater at all!'' Verity spoke the last words in some agitation, and rose suddenly from the sofa. "Do excuse me, Mama. I have a slight headache. I am going to my room.''

The countess directed a surprised look at her daughter, but Verity made no reply and hurried from the room. Lady Benbrook frowned. Something must be very wrong if Verity was saying she did not care about going to the theater. For years it had been her greatest passion. Her ladyship looked worried. It appeared that her daughter was not really reconciled to marrying Gerald after all. Lady Benbrook sighed and wished that she had a more staid and sensible daughter.

6

Nell Dawson skillfully pinned Verity's hair into a knot atop her head. She then worked on perfecting the short dark ringlets that framed the young lady's face. When she had finished, both mistress and maid studied Verity's reflection in the mirror. "I do think it looks very nice, don't you, my lady?"

Verity nodded, but without her usual enthusiasm. "Yes, thank you, Nell."

"Would you be wanting your pearl comb? That would do nice with your earrings. I could fasten it here at the side. Or two satin bows might be better."

"Oh, Nell, there is no necessity for anything further. I look sufficiently presentable as I am. We are only going to the theater."

This was said in such a disheartened manner that Nell frowned. "Oh, my lady, I cannot bear that you are so sad."

"Dear Nell, I do not mean to distress you," said Verity, turning away from the mirror and rising from her dressing table. "It is only that the theater has lost its appeal to me.

I shall not be able to watch a play without thinking how presumptuous I was to think I could write a drama. Going to the theater is only a reminder of how utterly silly I have been.''

''My lady,'' cried Nell, ''that is not true. I do wish you had not taken what that horrible Lord Ranley said so to heart. He is a very stupid man, and an unkind one. I wish I were a man. Then I should demand he apologize or I would call him out.''

''Oh, Nell,'' said Verity, bursting into laughter despite her unhappy mood. ''What a ridiculous thought. You dueling with Lord Ranley!'' Nell, happy at making her mistress laugh, smiled broadly. ''Well, I must be going, Nell. I fear I am late and my mother will be growing impatient. Where is my fan?'' The maid handed her mistress the fan and her gloves. ''Thank you, Nell.''

Verity left her room and joined her mother in the drawing room. The countess looked splendid in a gown of apricot silk. ''Oh, Mama, you do look wonderful.''

''Thank you, my dear. Why, Nell has done such a lovely job with your hair. I would have her do mine except Antoinette would make such a fuss. But you do look beautiful, Verity. I daresay none of the gentlemen will be watching the play. They will be watching you.''

''What nonsense, Mama,'' said Verity with a smile. She glanced at the mantel clock. ''And I am on time. But where is Gerald's carriage? I cannot imagine he is late.'' As the clock began to toll the hour, the butler appeared to announce Lord Dorchester.

That gentleman was always admirably punctual. ''Precisely on time,'' said Lady Benbrook as the marquess appeared in the drawing room. He escorted Verity and Lady Benbrook from the house to the carriage where the duchess was waiting.

''Good evening, my dears,'' said the duchess as the other ladies settled themselves in the carriage seat across from her.

''It is so exciting to be going to the theater again,'' said

Lady Benbrook. "It was so dull in Lancashire. I so longed to be in the thick of things once again."

"I do think the country is decidedly dull," agreed Dorchester as he climbed into the carriage and took the seat beside his mother. "Except for the hunting, of course."

"You gentlemen always enjoy hunting so much," said Lady Benbrook. "But it is not so exciting for the ladies, waiting about hoping that no one will break his neck over a fence."

"Yes," agreed the duchess. "I think the country holds few amusements for ladies. That is why we so enjoy town. And while Gerald does not like the theater, I must say I am looking forward to seeing this play."

"What is it called?" asked the countess.

"*Valiant Lady*," returned the duchess.

"I am sure it is just some absurd rubbish," said Dorchester. "Everyone is making such a great to-do over it simply because it was written by that fellow Ranley."

At the name Ranley, Verity, who had been staring absently out the carriage window at the darkened street, looked over at the marquess. "Written by Lord Ranley?"

"Oh, yes, his newest creation. I am sure it is sentimental tripe."

"Now, Gerald," said the duchess, "Lady Jersey told me it was a delightful play. She adored it."

"Oh, I am sure ladies will like it," said Dorchester in a tone that implied he did not have much faith in female judgment.

"I think Ranley is the most handsome man," said Lady Benbrook. "And so clever, too. I know Verity so admires him." To her mother's surprise, Verity made no reply to this remark.

"He was such a wonderful Brutus, and was not his Hamlet utterly splendid?" said the duchess. "And he is such an attractive man. Lady Jersey thinks him charming, but I cannot recollect ever having met him."

"Nor have I," said Lady Benbrook.

"I hardly think him suitable company for you ladies," said Dorchester.

"But, Gerald," said the countess, "he is from one of the oldest families. Oh, I know his reputation, but everyone is receiving him now."

"Well, I should not receive the likes of him," replied the marquess sourly. "And as to him being from one of the oldest families, why, yes, the Ranleys are respectable enough. But his mother was an actress. And she was Welsh or Irish or some such thing. And Ranley's father was tossed out by his family to make his living as an actor! Good heavens, I can scarcely imagine anything more shocking.

"And this Ranley lived as a common actor most of his life. And now that he has inherited his title, he moves about in Society as if he belongs there. He has taken a very grand house on Hanover Square and lives in a vulgar, extravagant fashion. They say he is always drunk. No, I have no desire to meet him. Indeed, I should love to have the opportunity to snub him."

Verity stared at her fiancé in silence, wondering whether Ranley or Dorchester was more insufferable. "I cannot believe you are not defending Lord Ranley, Verity," said Lady Benbrook with a smile. "I know you are such a great admirer of his. Remember when you were sixteen and we saw him in that play by Mrs. Sheffield? I forget the name of it. You could speak of nothing else for weeks."

"I was very young then, Mama," said Verity severely. "I am two and twenty and I no longer can be dazzled by an actor mouthing inanities."

The countess was quite shocked by this uncharacteristic response, but Dorchester looked very pleased. "My dear Verity, how sensible of you. I can see you are no longer a silly little girl. Yes, I am very glad to see it. But I do wish we would talk of something else beside Ranley. He is an insignificant, ill-bred fellow and an improper topic for ladies."

Verity found herself irked by Dorchester's pompous tones, but she only looked outside at the dimly lit streets. The duchess and Lady Benbrook began discussing the son of a mutual acquaintance and Verity tried to listen. She was glad when they arrived at the theater where the crowd and bustle of activity would take her mind off her unhappiness.

The Queen's Theater was ablaze with light and there was an atmosphere of intense excitement about the place. There was a crush of people and carriages as theatergoers arrived. It was some time before Dorchester's fashionable phaeton was able to deposit its illustrious passengers. The marquess eyed the multitude that flocked inside the theater with disfavor. There were a great many persons of quality about, to be sure, but to his lordship's eye, there were far more of the common sort who would occupy the gallery or pit.

It was a great relief to Dorchester when he and the ladies were safely inside their box. The marquess noted with satisfaction that his was a very good box, advantageously located for the best view of the stage and the other boxes.

The theater was a magnificent place, teeming with activity. Brilliantly lit both before and during the performance, one could observe the members of the audience who talked noisily and stared at each other without the slightest embarrassment. It was a place to see and be seen and to flirt. Young bucks surveyed the boxes with opera glasses, shamelessly ogling the pretty girls. The ladies made much use of their opera glasses as well. Signaling their admirers with their fans, they hoped that their husbands would not notice.

Verity gazed down at the throng below her with a cool expression. Usually she could not contain her excitement at attending a play. She did not meet the gazes of the numerous gentleman who were glancing in her direction. Instead, she glanced down at the playbill in her hand and studied it intently. Mrs. Fleming was playing a character named Princess Flavia. She looked at the list of supporting players and was struck with an odd coincidence. A number of the characters had the same names as those in *The Warrior Princess*.

On the opposite side of the theater another party entered a box and sat down. The group consisted of two elegantly dressed ladies and three gentlemen. One of the gentlemen was Lord Ranley. Although his companions were quite merry, the baron was in a rather glum mood. "What is the matter with you, Ranley?" said a tall young gentleman sitting beside his lordship. "You are dashed gloomy tonight. This play is a great triumph for you."

"Yes," said Ranley absently. He looked about the crowd and found himself wishing he had a glass of brandy.

The man seated next to him, whose name was Sir Robert Jeffries, grinned. "What a damned lot of good looking women."

"Robert," said the lady sitting next to him, a lovely blonde in a blue dress and matching turban, "you would do well to keep away from the ladies."

"That is impossible, my dear sister." Jeffries laughed good naturedly and continued to scan the crowd. "Who is that young lady sitting with the Duchess of Haverford?"

The blond lady directed her opera glasses in the direction her brother was looking. "Why, that is Verity de Lacy. She is to marry the Marquess of Dorchester. And that is her mother, Lady Benbrook."

"God, she is a stunner," said Jeffries. "Don't you think so, Ranley?"

The baron looked across the theater and his eyes alighted on the object of his companion's interest. "Yes, she is tolerable good looking," returned Ranley with studied indifference. In truth, he was quite taken with Verity's appearance. There was something about her as she sat there looking at her program, ignoring the commotion about her. He was not certain what it was, but he continued to glance in her direction whenever he was sure that Jeffries was not watching him.

Unaware of the interest she had provoked in Lord Ranley,

Verity looked up from her program and studied the people milling about below them. "Why I believe that is Ranley over there," said the Duchess of Haverford. "He is sitting with Sir Robert Jeffries and his sister, Lady Newbridge."

Verity looked across into the boxes opposite them. She was acquainted with Lady Newbridge and found her immediately. She then spotted Lord Ranley, who was talking to another gentleman. Verity had seen Ranley on the stage some years ago and he appeared unchanged. He was remarkably handsome, with a wild romantic appearance that made women swoon. Verity found herself growing increasingly indignant. How casually he had written the letter which had torn her heart to pieces. How easily he had shattered her very existence.

She frowned and stared at him. Suddenly he looked in her direction and their eyes met. Ranley was surprised to see that the young lady he had been studying now looked at him with such fierce disapproval.

At that moment the curtain rose and a somewhat disconcerted Ranley turned his attention to the stage. Verity continued to watch the baron until the opening speech of the play made her look at the stage in surprise. Why, this was very much like the beginning of *The Warrior Princess*, she thought. As the actors continued, Verity looked bewildered. It *was* the beginning of *The Warrior Princess*, word for word.

Mrs. Fleming appeared on the stage to great cheers and applause. When the racket had died down, she began to speak in her famous contralto voice the lines Verity had written for her own Princess Thalia.

For a moment Verity was too stunned to think. Then the reality came to her. Ranley had stolen her play! He had put his name on it! And to make the crime even more intolerable, he had sent her a letter telling her that she had no talent. Verity looked across at Ranley. Rage boiled inside her. How dare he do such a thing! A line of Princess Thalia's came to her. "By all the gods, he will pay for this outrage!"

Ranley watched the play, a look of keen interest on his

face. After a time, he cast a glance over at Verity. He had not expected to find her staring at him and he was totally unprepared to find her eyeing him with a look of unmistakable hatred. The baron sat up in his chair and looked at her in confusion.

Verity's face grew red. She wanted to shake her fist and shout at him. She wanted to rush from her box to his and strangle him. If only she had the spear that Princess Thalia, or Princess Flavia as they called her, was carrying about the stage. She would heave it across the auditorium and impale Lord Ranley with it. Yes, that would be a properly dramatic flourish.

But in reality, all Verity could do was sit in silence glaring at him, her outrage growing with every line that was spoken on the stage. She wondered how long she could endure sitting there.

Verity's mind raced. What could she do? No one knew she was a playwright. They would think her mad if she claimed she had written this play. No, she must somehow calm herself.

"Is it not thrilling?" whispered Lady Benbrook, leaning toward her daughter.

"Yes, Mama," Verity managed to say. She looked across at Lord Ranley with an expression worthy of Princess Thalia and sat in grim silence.

7

Nell Dawson had spent a pleasant evening in the servant's hall, knitting and conversing with Weeks, the butler, and Antoinette, Lady Benbrook's maid. Antoinette was a never-ending source of gossip, always regaling her listeners with the most entertaining and oftentimes shocking stories. Although Weeks feigned disapproval of discussing one's betters, he made no attempt to stop his coworker from telling them what she had heard of this highborn lady or that well-known gentleman.

The time seemed to fly by and it did not seem very long before the ladies returned from the theater. Nell eagerly answered the bell that rang from Verity's room, for she always enjoyed hearing about a new play. She also hoped that the excitement of a night at the theater would help bring Verity out of her doldrums. As the maid entered her mistress's room, Nell knew at once from Verity's expression that something was wrong.

"Oh, Nell!" cried Verity. "You cannot know what I have endured!"

"My lady, what has happened?"

"Oh, Nell, something too dreadful! I have been very badly used by a gentleman."

"My lady! Not Lord Dorchester! What did he do?"

"Oh, Nell, not Dorchester. I am speaking of Ranley. He has stolen my play. Yes, he has taken *The Warrior Princess* and put his name to it. I have just spent the most wretched evening watching my own play performed. And I was not completely happy with the performance, I might add. Can you imagine what it was to suffer through this in silence? And the despicable rogue Ranley sat across from us, happy to take the acclaim given to my play."

"This is horrible, my lady," said Nell. "But you are certain it was the same play?"

"Hardly a word was changed." Verity sat down on her bed and motioned for Nell to sit beside her. "And to think that this Ranley sent me a letter, telling me that I had no ability. No wonder that he did not return my play to me. He obviously felt that I was so insignificant that he could steal my play with impunity." There was a cold gleam in Verity's eye. "By my honor, Nell, this Ranley will see how wrong he was to think he could best Verity de Lacy."

Nell grew a little worried at her mistress's words. "But what will you do, my lady?"

"I am not sure, but I will do something." Verity looked thoughtful. "I think we will go and see Baron Ranley tomorrow."

"Oh, my lady, you couldn't think to call on him. Not alone."

"I shall have you with me, Nell."

"But do you think it wise, my lady? Why just this evening Antoinette was saying that Lord Ranley was a very . . ." Nell hesitated to select the right word. "A very improper gentleman. And to think that he would steal your play! Why, he is not gentleman at all, but a blackguard. No, indeed, my lady, it will not do calling on such a one as that. Perhaps you might speak to Lord Benbrook or Lord Dorchester."

"Don't be a goose, Nell. I can hardly tell them of this. I daresay they would not believe me. And could you imagine Gerald learning that I write plays? He would be appalled. Not that I care one fig for what he thinks."

"But you are to marry him, my lady."

"What does that signify?" said Verity. "No, I shall deal with this myself." Verity rose from the bed. "Do help me undress now, Nell. I should go to bed, although I cannot imagine how I shall ever sleep. It was a dreadful experience, Nell."

"I can see that it was, my lady," said Nell, beginning to unbutton the tiny mother-of-pearl buttons at the back of Verity's gown. "But, my lady, there was a good side of it."

Verity looked back at her maid. "What was that?"

"Why, Lord Ranley must have liked your play very much to steal it."

Verity smiled. "I suspect you are right, Nell. Yes, that is a very good point. And it is a great success."

"And that should make your ladyship feel much better."

"Yes, I suppose it should," agreed Verity as Nell continued unfastening the buttons.

Rising early the next morning, Verity summoned Nell. Despite the worthy servant's caution that her mistress not act hastily, Verity was more than ever resolved to call upon Ranley and confront him about his treachery.

Verity dressed and went downstairs, deciding to go on her mission before her parents were up. She knew that it would be some time before either Lord or Lady Benbrook would leave their bedchambers, for they usually did not appear before eleven while in town. After breakfasting on toast and hot chocolate, Verity informed Nell that they would go out at once.

Nell, although filled with misgivings, could only nod and fetch their bonnets and wraps. Lady Benbrook's lapdog, Jackanapes, having come down early to beg for scraps from Verity's plate, was to accompany them, for Verity felt taking

the little creature on a walk was a good excuse for leaving
the house.

"If her ladyship comes down, Weeks, tell her that we have
taken Jackanapes out," said Verity. "I do not know how
long we will be gone, but it seems a pleasant day for a walk."

"Her ladyship will be very pleased that the little fellow
has a good walk, my lady," said Weeks.

The two young women and the dog left the house and
started off down the sidewalk. Verity held firmly to
Jackanapes's leash and the little creature pranced along,
ecstatic to be out. Jackanapes was a small black long-haired
dog with a plumed tail. He had perky pointed ears and a
foxlike countenance that gave him a clever sprightly aspect.
Verity was very fond of him, although he was mischievous
and dreadfully spoiled by Lady Benbrook.

"Is it very far, my lady?" asked Nell.

"Less than a mile," returned Verity. "Dorchester
mentioned last night that Lord Ranley has a house on Hanover
Square. I am well acquainted with the location."

Nell was happy that her mistress apparently knew where
she was going. However, Nell thought their calling upon
Ranley a very bad idea. She knew it was useless to say
anything to Verity, for the young lady had clearly decided
upon this course of action. Nell knew well that there were
few young ladies more stubborn and determined than Verity
de Lacy.

It did not take long before they arrived at Hanover Square
with its imposing townhouses and a lovely park in the center
of the square. Verity hailed a baker's boy, who was deliver-
ing bread to one of the houses. "Young man, would you
please tell me which house is Lord Ranley's?"

The boy, a skinny unkempt fellow, nodded and stared at
Verity. "That one, miss," he said, pointing. "Just two doors
from here."

"Thank you very much," said Verity, pleased at so easily
locating Ranley's residence. She pulled a coin from her

reticule and gave it to the boy. He thanked her profusely and scurried off. "That was easy enough, Nell."

"Aye, my lady, but are you sure it is a good idea to see Lord Ranley? Perhaps we should go home."

"Nell, do not be so faint-hearted. There is nothing to be afraid of. Come along."

The maid could only suppress a sigh and follow Verity as she and the little black dog made their way to Ranley's door. There was a wolf's head door knocker affixed there, which Nell thought rather ominous. Verity did not hesitate, but scooping up the little dog Jackanapes into her arms, she rapped firmly against the door with the brass knocker.

In a few moments, a tall butler appeared. He eyed Verity, Nell, and Jackanapes curiously. "Yes, madam?"

"I should like to see Lord Ranley."

"I am sorry, madam, but Lord Ranley has not yet risen."

"I shall wait for him then." To the butler's great surprise, Verity pushed by him and walked boldly into the house. "I must speak to him on a matter of great urgency. I suggest you inform him at once that I am here."

Ranley's butler eyed Verity in confusion, unsure of how to react. This young lady was obviously a person of quality, he decided. That was apparent by the fashionable pelisse and bonnet she wore as well as her way of speaking. The lady's commanding tone of voice and regal manner made it difficult to argue with her.

"Indeed, miss, it may be a very long time before his lordship—"

Verity cut him off abruptly. "I have said I am here on a matter of great importance." She adopted a haughty pose. "Inform Lord Ranley that I am here. Do so at once."

"May I have your name, madam?"

"No, you may not," said Verity curtly. "Simply tell your master that a lady has serious business with him."

The man hesitated, but was cowed by Verity's icy gaze. "Very well, ma'am. If you will wait in the drawing room."

When he had gone, Verity handed Jackanapes to Nell. "I hope he will not be long." Looking about the room, Verity noted that it was decorated in an Egyptian motif with mauve walls decorated with a border of papyrus flowers. Enormous fans of ostrich feathers decorated the fireplace.

Verity sat down on a sofa and Nell joined her. "My lady, Lord Ranley may refuse to see us."

"He will see us if we have to drag him from his bed ourselves," said Verity resolutely.

Nell eyed her mistress with admiration. She was so calm and brave while Nell was quite timorous. She clutched Jackanapes tightly to her. Yet for all her bravado, Verity was in truth rather nervous sitting there waiting for Ranley. After all, he was a gentleman of considerable substance, a man whom she had until a few days ago held in great esteem. Verity frowned and hoped that he would not keep them waiting long.

Lord Ranley was downing a glass of port from a decanter in his room as his butler entered. "What is it, Huntley?"

"There are two young ladies here to see your lordship."

"Here at this hour? Good God, man, did you not send them on their way?" Ranley eyed his servant disapprovingly. He had often been plagued by lovestruck females calling upon him at the most inappropriate times. In earlier days, he had been amused and flattered, but now the excessive adulation he inspired in the fair sex most often annoyed him.

"I beg your pardon, my lord, but the young lady was not easily turned away. She is a very fine lady, by the look of her. She said it was very urgent."

"Oh, they all think it is very urgent," muttered Ranley. "What is her name?"

"She would not say, my lord, but she is very young and very pretty. I should think she is not much past one and twenty. She has very dark hair and blue eyes."

"I cannot imagine who she is," said Ranley. "Do send

her away, Huntley. I have no desire to listen to another moon-struck schoolgirl telling me how she adores my plays."

"If I may say so, my lord, this young lady did not look as if that was her business. She did not look very happy."

"Not look very happy?" Ranley thought immediately of the dark-haired young woman who had spent the previous evening glaring at him. Her name was Lady Verity de Lacy, and he had been told that she was a wealthy and privileged young woman who was engaged to marry the heir to a duke-dom. Could it be she? No, he told himself. He was ridiculously obsessive, thinking of her that morning. "Well, perhaps I shall see this young lady, Huntley. Have Tucker come to me."

"Very good, my lord," said the butler, very much relieved that he did not have to tell the formidable young woman in the drawing room that she would have to go. He hurried to call Ranley's valet and then reappeared in the drawing room where he announced to Verity and Nell that the baron would join them as soon as possible.

"You see, Nell? He will see us."

"Yes, my lady," said Nell rather surprised.

"If he keeps us cooling our heels, I shall be even more infuriated with him," said Verity. "But I shall wait all day if necessary." She got up from the sofa and paced across the room. Jackanapes jumped from Nell's lap and followed her.

Nell said nothing, but sincerely hoped that Ranley would appear soon. After fifteen minutes, Nell could see that Verity was losing patience for she continued to pace, her frown deepening with each minute. Fortunately, a short time later, Ranley appeared at the door.

He was, Verity found herself thinking, an infuriatingly handsome man. He stood there, elegantly dressed, his dark eyes regarding them with apparent indifference. Ranley recognized Verity immediately and it took considerable self-control not to express the interest the sight of her registered within him. She was a very attractive young lady, he decided, although the expression she was directing at him was far from friendly.

"Good morning, ladies," said the baron, entering the drawing room. "I am Ranley. I am told you have some business with me."

"I do indeed, my lord," said Verity, viewing him with disfavor. Jackanapes, sensing Verity's feelings, yapped and snarled. She picked him up and handed him back to Nell, who had risen from the sofa at the appearance of the baron.

"Do sit down, ladies," said Ranley politely. When they were seated, he took a place in an exotic-looking armchair and waited expectantly.

"My name is Lady Verity de Lacy. This is my companion, Miss Dawson."

"Your servant, ladies," returned the earl, wondering what on earth the lovely and clearly unhappy Lady Verity was doing there.

"I expect that now that you know my name, you are well aware of why I have come, Lord Ranley."

The baron looked puzzled. "I confess I do not, Lady Verity. I should be most obliged if you would enlighten me."

Verity found his bland pleasantness particularly maddening. "Do not pretend with me, my lord. Did you believe you could wrong me in this way and that I would say nothing?"

Ranley regarded her in astonishment. "My dear lady, I have never before met you. I cannot imagine how I have offended you. And I daresay, had I wronged you in the way a gentleman most often wrongs a pretty girl, I should remember it very well."

Verity reddened in embarrassment. "You are insufferable, sir," she cried. "You know well enough that you have stolen my play, *The Warrior Princess,* which I sent to you some weeks ago asking you to read. You then sent me a letter saying I had no ability and then you took the play as your own, calling it *Valiant Lady.* I truly believe there is nothing more comtemptible than what you have done to me."

Ranley stared at her seemingly uncomprehending. "Your play?" he said finally. "You sent me a play?"

"Yes, of course, I did. Do not pretend that you do not know what I am speaking of, my lord. I can prove what I say. I have a copy of *The Warrior Princess* at my home in Lancashire. And Nell read it as I wrote it."

Ranley stared in disbelief. He now had a vague recollection of a play arriving from Lancashire. Of course, people were often sending him plays and dreadful novels to read. An awful ray of enlightenment came to him suddenly. So this is how Billy Hawkins had got the play! "My God," said Ranley. "It was your play. You must believe I knew nothing about it."

"You knew nothing about it?" said Verity. "Come, come, Lord Ranley, how could you know nothing about this?"

The baron rose to his feet. "You have my abject apology, Lady Verity. You see, I am guilty of great stupidity, but no villainy in this matter. I pray you will excuse me, for I will get to the bottom of this. Good day to you."

"Wait a moment, sir," said Verity, hurrying to her feet. "Where are you going?"

"I am going to seek an explanation for this damnable business."

"But it is I who must have an explanation, and from you," cried Verity. "And I will not leave here without one. What you have said makes no sense. You cannot expect me to believe you are blameless? That is preposterous!"

"As I have said, Lady Verity, I shall get your explanation."

"Do not think that you may run away from me, my lord," said Verity.

This remark clearly irritated the baron. "I am not running away from you, my lady. I am going to the Queen's Theater where I will investigate this matter. Perhaps you would like to accompany me?"

Verity looked into Ranley's eyes. "Yes, I fancy that I would wish to do so."

"Very well, come along. Huntley! Have the carriage brought around, and quickly!"

"Oh, my lady," said Nell. "You cannot mean to go with Lord Ranley."

"I do indeed, Nell. Now come along."

A worried expression on her face, Nell rose from the sofa and, Jackanapes held tightly in her arms, she followed Verity and Ranley from the room.

8

Nell Dawson thought her mistress rash and foolish to accompany Ranley in his carriage, considering that gentleman's reputation. Whatever would happen if someone saw her? Although Verity appeared unconcerned, she was not oblivious to the folly of being seen with Lord Ranley, for she was well aware that respectable unmarried ladies did not ride about town with men they scarcely knew.

"I would appreciate it if you would put the hood of your carriage up, Lord Ranley," said Verity as the baron's groom brought the vehicle round to the front of the house.

"That would be prudent," replied Ranley, commanding his groom to do so. He then assisted Verity and Nell into the equipage. Once they were inside, the baron frowned at the ladies who were seated across from him. "This is a most disconcerting kettle of fish."

"If it is disconcerting to you, Lord Ranley, you can imagine what I felt to discover that you had stolen my play."

"Do not say that. I assure you I have done nothing of the kind."

"Yes, that is what you claim," said Verity. "Well, I shall wait to hear this explanation you have promised me. I hope you will know how mortified I was to attend the theater last night completely unaware that I was to see the very play that I had written. I could scarcely believe it. And then to see you sitting across from me gloating."

"I was not gloating," replied Ranley testily. "So that is why you regarded me like a wronged she-wolf all evening."

"She-wolf? I hardly think I deserve an insult from you considering the circumstances."

"I only meant that you looked very angry. I kept wondering why."

Verity regarded him scornfully. "I had very good reason to be angry."

"Indeed you did," said Ranley. "No, this is an unfortunate matter. I shall do all I can to rectify it."

Although Verity did not appear convinced of this, she said nothing. The dog Jackanapes seemed very pleased to be riding in a carriage and sat there on Nell's lap staring at Ranley. The baron frowned and looked out the window, glad that the trip to the Queen's Theater was a short one.

When they arrived, Ranley assisted Verity and Nell down and escorted them inside. "Milord Brutus!" cried a familiar voice.

"Jenkins," said the baron. "Where is Mr. Hawkins?"

"In the office, my lord." Jenkins eyed the ladies appreciatively, thinking Ranley had very good taste in women.

"This way, ladies," said his lordship, motioning them forward.

Arriving at Hawkins's office, the baron knocked once on the door and opened it. William Hawkins was sitting at his desk, sifting through a stack of papers. He looked up in surprise. "Brutus? Here at this hour?" Seeing Verity and Nell, he jumped to his feet and smiled. "What a pleasure. Welcome, ladies."

"I fear it may not be a pleasure, Billy," said Ranley. "Not when you hear what has brought these ladies to see you."

"I cannot believe that," said Hawkins. "Ladies, do come in and sit down."

Nell and Verity seated themselves in wooden chairs near the desk. The baron remained standing. "I shall make the introductions. Lady Verity de Lacy and Miss Dawson, this is Mr. Hawkins, manager of the Queen's Theater."

"A very great honor, ladies," said Hawkins bowing to them. He grinned, but suddenly experienced a sinking feeling. Lady Verity de Lacy? V. de Lacy? Of Lancashire?

"Lady Verity has come to me with a story," said Ranley. "Perhaps I should say an accusation, which places me in a very unfavorable light, Billy. It makes me look the worst sort of knave imaginable."

"I don't know what you could possibly mean," said Hawkins. He noted with alarm that Ranley's color was rising.

"Lady Verity has accused me of stealing her play."

"My dear lady," said Hawkins, "his lordship would not do such a thing."

This remark caused the baron to lose his temper. In two steps he was beside Hawkins, roughly grabbing the lapels of his well-tailored coat. "Dammit, Billy. You are found out! You took the lady's play from my house. Confess it, you rapscallion, or you will rue the day you were born!"

"Yes, Brutus, very well. I confess everything."

Releasing his grip on Hawkins, Ranley looked over at Verity. "So you see, Lady Verity. I did not take your play."

"But you did not prevent Mr. Hawkins from doing so, Lord Ranley," said Verity severely.

"But I had no idea that he had done so," said Ranley. "Explain it to her, Billy."

Hawkins shrugged and smoothed out the front of his coat. "You see, my lady, I am guilty. I stand before you admitting my shame. Oh, what I did was unforgiveable." Hawkins fixed a dejected expression upon her ladyship and clasped his hands together as if begging for mercy. It had been some years since Billy Hawkins had trod the boards, but his present speech was becoming as theatrical as any he had delivered upon the stage. "I was driven to it, my lady," he cried, directing a tragic look at Ranley. "I am not a wealthy man and I have such great expenses with the theater. His lordship promised me a play. Without it I would be ruined!"

"What rubbish," muttered Ranley. "You have never been richer, Billy."

"Do allow Mr. Hawkins to continue," said Verity, greatly interested in what the theater manager was saying.

"You are so kind, my lady. Lord Ranley had no play. He had not written even one word of it. And I do not like to say this of my dear friend Ranley, but he was in his cups. Yes, he fell asleep while I was there. And then I came upon your wonderful play. It was exactly what I needed, but, you see, I needed a Ranley play. Everyone demanded it. Why, I was threatened with riot if I did not have a new play by Brutus Ranley. So what could I do? I took your play. I can only beg that you will forgive me."

Verity nodded slowly. "I think I understand what happened, but I shall not be so quick to forgive you, Mr. Hawkins. You did write that letter to me, did you not? Saying I should abandon playwriting?"

Hawkins reddened. "I cannot deny it."

Verity seemed to consider this. "But what I don't understand is why Lord Ranley allowed you to perpetrate this deception. I find it unconscionable that you did so, sir."

"But I did not do so. I did not know it was your play."

"No, he did not," said Hawkins. "I convinced his lordship that he dictated the play to me when he was drunk. He thought he had simply forgotten."

Verity's blue eyes opened wide in surprise. She looked over at the baron, who had reddened in obvious embarrassment. To Ranley's surprise she burst into laughter. Nell looked at her mistress and then the baron and joined in, while Hawkins grinned and then guffawed.

"Forgive me, Lord Ranley," Verity finally managed to say, "but it is too funny."

"I do not appreciate being thought ridiculous, madam," said Ranley ominously.

"No, of course not," said Verity, trying to appear serious. "It is not really funny at all. I do see that I must hold you blameless, Lord Ranley."

"And you will forgive me, will you not, Lady Verity?" said Hawkins hopefully.

"I don't know, sir," returned Verity. "I daresay I have been sorely wronged and although you admit your guilt, the matter has hardly been solved to my satisfaction."

"I shall make a public statement saying that you are the author," said Ranley. "That will settle things."

"Oh, I don't know that I want that," said Verity quickly.

"You don't?" said Hawkins much relieved.

"Why, my father would be very upset. And Lord Dorchester would be furious. Since I am to marry Lord Dorchester, I suppose I must take into account his feelings. He abhors the theater, you see. No, I do not imagine revealing the fact that I am the author would be the thing to do."

"Then what would you wish us to do?" said Ranley. "Would you think it fitting if both of us jumped into the Thames?"

Verity grinned. "I should like to see that, but I am not so heartless."

"Perhaps your ladyship might be agreeable to a financial settlement?" ventured Hawkins.

"Financial settlement?" Verity regarded him with interest. She never gave much thought to money since her father had always been overly generous, allowing her to buy whatever she wished. Still, the idea of having one's own resources seemed appealing. Verity pondered this for a moment and then looked at Hawkins. "How much?"

Ranley nearly let out an exclamation at this, but he caught himself. Saying that Lady Verity de Lacy was a mercenary baggage like any other female would have hardly helped matters.

Hawkins eyed Verity warily. He was a shrewd business-
man who hated parting with a shilling. "Fifty pounds," he
said finally.

Verity looked over at Ranley. "I know nothing of these
things. Would you consider that fair compensation, Lord
Ranley?"

The baron shook his head. "No, I do not. I should think
one hundred pounds more like it, Billy."

"Do you want to ruin me, Brutus?"

"God in heaven, you are getting off damned easy."

"Oh, very well, Lady Verity. One hundred. But it is now
Ranley's play."

"Yes, I shall agree to that. However . . ."

"However what?" said Hawkins fearfully.

"However, I do think there should be a few changes in
the performance."

"What?" cried Hawkins.

"I was quite unhappy with Act One," continued Verity.
"They are not very big changes, Mr. Hawkins, and I will
be most obliged if you could make them."

"Very well," said Hawkins. "But I think this most
irregular."

"I think it all very irregular," said Verity, bursting once
again into laughter.

When some time later, Ranley escorted Verity and Nell
from the theater, a passerby on a horse caught sight of them
and appeared startled. Mr. Charles Allenby, a member of
the dandy set and well-known hanger-on in Society, quickly
took up his quizzing glass and studied the well-dressed young
lady as Ranley handed her up into the carriage.

"Who is that lady?" Allenby asked himself. Why, it
looked like the de Lacy girl who was to marry the Marquess
of Dorchester. Allenby decided he must be mistaken until
he noted Nell Dawson and the little black dog she was carrying. Allenby was well acquainted with Jackanapes, since
Lady Benbrook was so often seen with him. A broad smile

appeared on Allenby's face. Lady Verity de Lacy and Ranley, he thought. What a delicious bit of gossip. He continued on his way, and as he glanced back at Ranley's departing carriage, he smiled a very self-satisfied smile.

9

Returning home, Lord Ranley slumped down into his favorite armchair in the library and sat reflecting upon his new acquaintance with Lady Verity de Lacy. She was, he decided, a very strong-minded young lady, and doubtless her father had his hands full with her. She was deuced pretty, too, thought the baron. Pity she thought him utterly ridiculous.

Ranley frowned. He was accustomed to the adoration of females. Indeed, most young ladies were apt to swoon at the least of his attentions. It had been a sobering experience to be with a young woman who appeared immune to his charm. Indeed, reflected Ranley, Lady Verity had first thought him a bounder, and now considered him a fool.

The memory of Verity's laughter was especially painful to his lordship, for he could think of few things worse than being thought ridiculous. Well, the baron told himself, he had been an idiot to allow Billy Hawkins to bamboozle him into thinking he had dictated a play while drunk. Lady Verity was right to think him the greatest grudgeon.

Frowning again, Ranley told himself that at least that was the end of it. After all, in all likelihood, he would see little or nothing of Verity de Lacy again. Yet still, he would be constantly reminded of his own stupidity each time the play *Valiant Lady* would be mentioned and he would have to continue in the deceit of allowing people to believe he had written it.

Folding his arms across his chest, Ranley looked grim. This would not have happened if he had written a play for Hawkins. Nor would it have happened if he had not been stinking drunk. He rose from his chair and walked across the room to the window. There he stood gazing out at the street, a thoughtful expression on his face.

Verity was very glad that they had arrived home just before her parents came down for breakfast. Lady Benbrook was very pleased to hear that her daughter had taken Jackanapes for a walk. Her ladyship believed firmly in the value of daily exercise, although she herself seldom found the time for such activity. The earl and countess were also happy to see that their daughter appeared in such good spirits.

As Verity sat at the breakfast table, she realized that she had had a quite extraordinary day. Although it was scarcely past eleven o'clock, she had already bravely confronted the famous Lord Ranley and had discovered the truth about the unscrupulous Mr. Hawkins. What was even more remarkable was that she had sold her play for a large sum of money. Since Verity was nearly bursting with the news, it was almost unendurable remaining silent on the subject.

"I do hope Jackanapes was no trouble to you, Verity," said the countess, taking a morsel of food from her plate and feeding it to her eager canine friend.

"Oh, no, Mama. Jack was quite good. We had a very nice walk."

"Weeks said you were out early, my dear," said the earl. "I do hope you do not tire yourself. You ladies were out very late at the theater. You must tell me all about the play."

"My dear Benbrook," said the countess. "You missed a wonderful performance. I have scarcely ever enjoyed myself more. Did you not think it was a very good play, Verity?"

"Oh, yes," replied Verity with a smile. "I thought it very good indeed."

"And Mrs. Fleming was so very inspiring," said Lady Benbrook. "Oh, yes, Benbrook, you were very silly to go to your club when you might have gone with us."

"But you know that I share Dorchester's view of the theater," replied the earl. "He and I both find it dull. But do tell me, Verity, if you and Dorchester spoke of your wedding date."

"We hardly spoke of anything, Papa. Conversation is not one of Gerald's strong points."

"Come, come, my girl, was the subject not even mentioned?"

"Indeed, it was not, Papa."

"Do not worry, Benbrook," said the countess. "I told the duchess that we would call upon them this afternoon. It will be a good opportunity to settle things. Dorchester and the duke will be there. I do hope you will accompany us."

"I shall do so," said the earl. "I believe the duke and I have come to a very equitable agreement over the marriage, but I shall be glad to have a few details settled."

Lady Benbrook nodded. "Yes, I fancy we will all be happy when the arrangements have been made."

Verity said nothing. The idea of facing her marriage to Dorchester depressed her. It was dreadful to have such a wonderful day spoiled with thoughts of her wedding. Why did she have to get married anyway? It was horrible that her own wishes were so totally ignored.

Verity controlled herself with some difficulty. There would be no point in antagonizing her parents, she reasoned. After all, she had said she would marry Dorchester, and she could scarcely say that she had changed her mind. No, she must reconcile herself to her fate, like some character in a tragic drama.

As Verity took a bite of her boiled egg, she reflected that hers was an unfortunate situation. It occurred to her that her plight would make an excellent subject for a play. Of course, the idea of a young girl forced into a marriage by her parents was hardly an original plot idea. Still, it was a good one, and if she had the opportunity, she could get to work on a new play while in town. After all, she was now a professional playwright and she would doubtlessly be able to sell other works.

Verity's thoughts so occupied her that she scarcely was aware of her parents' breakfast conversation. At first opportunity she retreated to her room and rang for Nell. That young woman appeared quickly.

"Nell, I have an inspiration for another play."

"Do you, my lady?" said Nell, always impressed at the creative energies of her mistress.

"Yes, I do. I shall begin work at once. I did bring my writing paper. Do have someone sharpen some pens for me, Nell. I shall have a few hours to work, for I told Mama that I was very tired.

"Oh, Nell, I do wish I had brought some of the other plays from the castle. I daresay Hawkins would have bought them." Verity sat down at her desk and smiled at her maid. "I can scarcely believe what has happened. Everything is so changed. To think how I was so miserable thinking that Ranley hated my play!" Verity appeared suddenly thoughtful. "Do you think he did like it, Nell?"

"I should think so, my lady, if he thought he wrote it."

Verity laughed. "It was too funny, was it not? Remember the look on his face? The poor man. Well, I am very glad that I do not have to hate him any longer."

Nell looked a bit wistful. "Did you not think that he is the most handsome man?"

Verity shrugged. "He is handsome, but that is of little

significance to me. It is Ranley's genius that has always interested me.''

Nell eyed her mistress with some skepticism. "Then he does interest you, my lady?''

"Don't be a ninnyhammer, Nell. I think of Ranley as an artist. As a man, I daresay he has a great many faults. No, do not fear that I would fall in love with someone like Ranley.'' Verity sighed. "Indeed, I shall never fall in love at all, Nell. That would be the wisest course. After all, I shall be married to Gerald. But let us have no more of such talk. Do see to my pens, Nell.'' The maid nodded and departed, leaving Verity to muse about her new literary work.

The London home of the Duke of Haverford was an imposing structure built just after the Great Fire that had destroyed much of the city in the seventeenth century. The duke was a gentleman of the old order who believed that civilization in England had fallen to pieces late in the last century. His grace, therefore, clung to many of the old ways that had long since fallen out of fashion. He was partial to powdered wigs and satin knee breeches and thought modern-day ladies should have never given up their whalebone stays and wide skirts.

In his young days, the duke had been a bit of a rake and something of a hellion. This, however, had been a very long time ago. He had long since mended his ways and was now a respectable but decidedly curmudgeonly gentleman. Since his grace was at times a cantankerous individual, he and his son Dorchester might have been expected to quarrel. However, they got along surprisingly well, for the marquess deferred to his father in everything.

That afternoon, when Lord and Lady Benbrook and Verity arrived at the residence of the Duke and Duchess of Haverford, they were received with great enthusiasm by his grace. The duchess was also very pleased to see them. Dorchester, as was his way, was more subdued. He did direct one slight smile at Verity and ventured to remark that her bonnet was very becoming.

When everyone had taken their places in the ducal drawing room, the duchess called for tea to be served. Verity sat on a sofa beside her mother and looked about the room. It was large and dreary, without a trace of elegance or charm.

"It is such a pleasure to have you all here," said the duchess, smiling broadly.

"Yes, indeed," said the duke. He was a tall, thin man, about sixty years of age, with piercing blue eyes and florid countenance. He wore an aged wig that seemed rather worse for wear, but his suit of clothes were of a fashionable and recent cut. "I must say that it is a glad day for this family that our son Dorchester will wed your dear little Verity. Yes, 'tis a very glad day for us." Dorchester nodded solemnly, but ventured no remark. His father continued. "I believe your solicitor has spoken with mine, Benbrook, regarding the marriage settlement."

The earl nodded. "He has, Duke, although there are a few details we must discuss."

"Yes, yes," said the duke. "We will do so after tea. Then the ladies will excuse us. But let us speak of when the nuptials will occur. What say you, Benbrook? I do not think any more time should pass before they are wed."

"I heartily agree," said the earl, looking at his daughter. "I have told my daughter that she may choose the day. Verity, how will you reply to his grace?"

Verity looked from her father to the duke and then to Dorchester and the two ladies. All were awaiting her words expectantly. "I should think the twenty-seventh of June a very good day."

"The twenty-seventh of June?" said the duchess. "Why that is more than a month away."

The earl frowned. "There is no need to wait so long, Verity. All the arrangements can be easily made."

"Your father is right," said Dorchester. "My dear girl, we could be married within a fortnight."

"That's the spirit, Dorchester," said the duke. "What an eager lad he is. And one cannot blame him, with such a fair bride."

"Oh, it is not that I would not wish to be married at once," said Verity with a disingenuous smile. She hesitated, her mind racing for a reason for such a delay. "It is that I have consulted an astrologer and he is convinced that the twenty-seventh of June is the most auspicious day for Gerald and me to be married."

"You have consulted an astrologer?" said the earl, regarding her with incredulity.

"Why yes, I know you will all think me a silly, superstitious female. But my friend Carolyn Billingham suggested it in a letter. Carolyn puts great stock in such things. Not that I do, of course, but a bride does want things to be perfect. I wrote to the gentleman Carolyn advised me to contact. He said that our astrological signs would be in perfect agreement on the twenty-seventh of June."

"That is very interesting, Verity," said the countess. "But you never said anything about this to us before."

"Oh, I didn't want you to think me a silly witling, Mama."

Convinced that his wayward daughter was gammoning them, the earl frowned. "This is utter poppycock, Verity."

"You are too harsh, Benbrook," said the duke. "I think it very sound to make such consultations. Yes, it is wise to consider the position of the stars and planets when making an important decision. If Verity was advised to be married on the twenty-seventh of June, I should think that an excellent idea. It is not so very far away. What do you think, Dorchester?"

The marquess seemed to be mulling over the matter. He had hoped to be married as soon as possible. Aside from the obvious advantage of wedding an attractive young lady of good family, Dorchester would experience a substantial financial gain upon his marriage. In addition to Verity's marriage settlemen, the marquess would inherit a tidy fortune due to provisions of his maternal grandfather's will that stipulated a large sum would be bestowed upon him upon his marriage. He had already been put off by Verity for two years and he was growing impatient. Still, the twenty-seventh of June was not so very far off. "I should think that would suit well enough if that is what Verity wishes."

"Then we shall eagerly await that important date," said the duke. Verity smiled, glad that she had postponed the inevitable for a time anyway. "Now do tell me about the play you ladies and Dorchester saw last evening."

"Oh, that," said the marquess. "It was mildly diverting, but I cannot see why such a great fuss is being made of it."

Verity looked over at her fiancé and wished that she had had her fictional astrologer proclaim that their horoscopes were in complete opposition and marriage out of the question.

10

The following afternoon Verity accompanied her mother on a shopping expedition, visiting first the milliner's and then the glovemaker's. Despite Lady Benbrook's great difficulty in finding a new bonnet and her general dissatisfaction with the quality of gloves presented to her, Verity's mother remained in the best of moods. After all, her daughter was finally to be married and Verity, while appearing subdued, did not seem unhappy.

When they returned from their errands, Lady Benbrook called for tea. While they sat in the drawing room awaiting their refreshment, the countess sorted through the stack of invitations that had recently arrived. "Oh dear, Lady Cowper wants us for dinner Thursday next. I had promised Lydia Wemberley that we would dine there. I should not wish to refuse Lady Cowper. What is one to do?"

Verity picked up some of the invitations her mother had discarded and began to thumb through them. "There are so many, Mama. One cannot attend everything. Surely Lady Cowper would understand that you are promised elsewhere."

"Oh, she would indeed, but that is not the point. Is one to go to the Wemberleys' when one has an invitation from Lady Cowper? No, I shall have to make excuses to the Wemberleys. There is nothing else to be done."

Verity nodded absently as she studied the invitations. "Why, look, Mama, here is an invitation from Aunt Sarah for tomorrow evening."

"Yes, I do remember seeing that," said the countess. "I must send our regrets."

"But why, Mama? I know we were going to the opera tomorrow, but we could go another time. Aunt Sarah always has the most interesting and amusing company."

"I do not approve of such company, Verity. Your aunt fancies she has established a salon. She invites the most dreadful people—artists, foreigners, and freethinkers. Why, it is quite scandalous whom she admits. She has taken up poets and actors and all manner of unacceptable persons." Lady Benbrook shrugged. "That is what comes from marrying a Frenchman, I suppose."

"Oh, Mama," cried Verity. Of all her numerous relations, her mother's sister Sarah was her favorite. Sarah had displeased her family by eloping with a French marquis many years ago, but after disowning her for a time, the family had forgiven Sarah and taken her back. After all, her husband was the scion of one of the most noble houses of France and he was frightfully rich as well. His fortunes had suffered a good deal during the French Revolution, but he had retained sufficient wealth to live grandly in London.

"You know that I am fond of Sarah," continued Lady Benbrook, "but your father thinks she is a very bad influence. No, I do think it best to send our regrets."

"Oh, Mama, could you not do even one thing I wish to do? It would be great fun seeing Aunt Sarah. Her parties are never dull. Oh, please, Mama! Do say we can go."

Lady Benbrook hesitated. She really did not see any harm in accepting her sister's invitation even though the earl would disapprove. And Verity was, of late, being so very good about everything, acceding to her parents' wishes about marrying Dorchester. "Well, perhaps we could go to Sarah's. I would not wish her to think we are snubbing her. She is my sister, after all. Yes, we can go."

"That is so good of you, Mama," said Verity, very pleased at the idea of visiting her favorite relation.

"You must write to Dorchester immediately and invite him to go with us. He is expecting us at the opera, you know."

"Oh, Mama! Gerald will not wish to go."

"That does not signify. He need not accompany us if he does not wish to do so. But you must inform him of your plans."

Verity sighed. "Very well, Mama. I shall do so immediately after tea."

"Very good, my dear." Lady Benbrook smiled at her daughter's obedient reply and turned her attention once again to her letters.

Verity's aunt Sarah, the Marquise de Chamfort, fancied herself a great patroness of the arts. She took great pleasure in assisting struggling painters, composers, opera singers, and other artists. She had a particular fondness for poets and playwrights, whom she adored.

The Marquis de Chamfort was a very charming and obliging gentleman who supported his wife's enthusiasms. Although he considered London something of a cultural backwater, far inferior to his beloved Paris, the marquis was too well mannered to express this opinion. Instead, he did what he could to promote the arts and letters among the philistines of English society.

The de Chamforts' elegant London home was a gathering place for intellectuals and artists. Expatriot Frenchmen were often to be found there as well as an assortment of other nationalities. The marquis and marquise always had a bevy of houseguests, usually artistic and eccentric persons who were happy to partake of the de Chamforts' largesse for as long as possible.

Lady Benbrook thought that her elder sister had become a good deal too Frenchified. She knew that living on the continent for several years had accomplished the unfortunate transformation in Sarah's personality.

The marquise was aware that her family did not entirely approve of her, but she did not care very much about the opinions of her less enlightened family members. From time to time she sent invitations to her kinsmen, never expecting that they would accept. She was, therefore, quite pleased to receive a note from her sister, Lady Benbrook, saying that Lord Benbrook, Verity, and she would attend the salon.

That evening as her guests began to arrive, Sarah greeted them warmly. She was happy to see a number of her dearest friends as well as several new and interesting personages. Of all of the arrivals at the de Chamforts' door, none was more eagerly received than the famed Lord Ranley.

His lordship had been invited numerous times to the salon, but in the past, he had always declined. Knowing that it was quite a feather in her cap to have the famed playwright appear, the Marquise de Chamfort could hardly contain her joy at the sight of the baron's handsome face. She greeted him effusively. "My dear Lord Ranley! I am so delighted that you have honored us with your presence."

The baron bowed over Sarah's hand politely. He was slightly acquainted with the marquise, having met her upon several occasions. He thought her likeable enough, although perhaps a trifle too passionate in her enthusiasms. "How very good of you to invite me, ma'am," replied Ranley.

The baron's appearance had caused a sensation among the company, who pressed closer to see the famous playwright. The boldest came forward for introductions and soon his lordship was surrounded by a group of excited guests, clamoring for his attention.

The arrival of the Benbrook party, by comparison, generated little interest. Sarah, of course, was very pleased to see her sister and most particularly her niece, Verity. She embraced that young lady and kissed her on both cheeks. "My dear Verity, how beautiful you look."

Verity did indeed look lovely, dressed in an evening gown of peach sarsenet. The high-waisted creation was elegant in its simplicity. Around Verity's slender neck was a pearl necklace and satin ribbons adorned her coal-black tresses. "Thank you, Aunt Sarah. You look very lovely."

"Nonsense," replied the marquise self-deprecatingly, but in truth Sarah was proud of her appearance. At forty-five years of age, she retained much of the great beauty that had first attracted the Marquis de Chamfort. Tall and voluptuous, she looked very grand in her fashionable gown of rose-colored silk. Her hennaed curls were partially covered with a toque trimmed with ostrich feathers. "And dear Benbrook."

The earl nodded to his sister-in-law. "Good evening, Sarah." Although he did not dislike his wife's sister, Benbrook was not particularly happy to be at the salon. He did not like foreigners and he suspected that there would be a preponderance of them at the de Chamforts'. He looked around the drawing room, frowning slightly at the other guests.

"And Lord Dorchester, what a wonderful surprise to see you here." The marquise smiled brightly at Gerald, who bowed in a civil manner and muttered that he was so very pleased to be there.

Dorchester, like his prospective father-in-law, had not wanted to attend the affair. However, since Verity was going to be there, he thought it was his duty to accompany her. He did not like the thought of his future bride with such company as would be likely to congregate at the de Chamforts'. As everyone in society knew, there were apt to be all manner of unacceptable persons there. At least if he were present with her, he could reign in his oftentimes too exuberant fiancée.

Verity would have much preferred that Dorchester had

stayed away. It had been a great disappointment to receive his response to her note which said that he would be happy to come. Still, Verity was determined that the marquess's presence would not spoil her evening. Let him be a stick-in-the-mud, thought Verity. She would talk with whom she pleased and enjoy herself. She looked around the room, noting a great number of interesting looking people, most of whom she did not know. On one side of the room there was a swarm of guests all chattering excitedly and surrounding a gentleman whose back was turned to Verity.

"Aunt," said Verity, "pray tell me who that gentleman is—the one who has excited so much attention."

"Oh, my dear, you will not believe your good fortune. Why, that is Lord Ranley, the playwright." At that moment the baron turned and Verity caught sight of his famous profile. "What a coup to have him," continued the marquise. "Is he not the most handsome man you have ever seen?"

"He is very handsome," acknowledged Lady Benbrook, looking in Ranley's direction. The earl and Dorchester only frowned distastefully and thought that women were hopelessly silly creatures.

Verity smiled, thinking that it would be very amusing having Ranley here. She noted that he did not appear to be having a good time despite the adoring mostly feminine crowd that surrounded him. Verity would have liked to have joined Ranley's admirers, but Dorchester took her arm and propelled her to the opposite side of the room where he could have a better look at the gathering.

"I cannot think why you would wish to attend such a function as this," said Dorchester. "I hardly know a soul here. And see how they hang about that Ranley fellow as if he were the Prince Regent. Who is he anyway but a scribbler of bad plays?"

"Certainly not a scribbler of bad plays," returned Verity, a mischievous expression appearing on her face. "He did write *Valiant Lady.*"

"Precisely," returned the marquess.

Verity had an urge to plant a kick on Dorchester's well-clad shins, but she restrained her temper. "You are a poor judge of literature, Gerald."

"Perhaps," said the marquess. "I do not pretend to know anything about it, not like these friends of your aunt's. I daresay they think themselves veritable sages. And I do not mean to be critical, Verity, but I do fancy Lady De Chamfort a bit of a bluestocking."

"My aunt?"

"Yes," returned Dorchester. "I do not approve of females taking on literary airs. I'm told she writes poetry."

"Surely that is no fault."

"It is in my view," said the marquess solemnly. "In fact, I consider writing poetry a poor occupation even for a man."

Verity regarded him in some exasperation. Had she really agreed to marry him? Why, she had always thought Gerald rather a bore, but she had not realized how insufferable he could be. "Do not be ridiculous, Gerald," she said impatiently. "And I refuse to hang about away from everyone. I am going to see Lord Ranley."

"See here, Verity . . ." began the marquess, but Verity walked briskly away. He could only follow her, grumbling to himself.

Ranley fielded his admirers' questions, many of which to his chagrin, referred to his latest masterwork, *Valiant Lady*. He tried to divert attention to his other works, but this play seemed to particularly interest most of those in attendance.

The baron, intent on the crowd surrounding him, had not noticed Verity's entrance, nor did he note the fact that she and Dorchester had joined the others. She stood a little behind the baron, noting the expressions of awed hero worship on the faces of Ranley's listeners.

"I do wish you would tell us more of how you were inspired to write *Valiant Lady*," said a smiling matron near the baron.

"There is nothing to say about that, ma'am," replied Ranley.

"Oh, do not be so modest, Lord Ranley," Verity's voice startled the baron, who turned his head to see her. It took all his lordship's considerable self-control to keep from expressing the surprise he felt at finding her there. "Do tell us how you came to write what many call your greatest play."

"My greatest play is yet to be written, madam," replied Ranley, casting a warning look at Verity.

"Spoken like a true artist," said Verity. "But surely you think *Valiant Lady* your greatest work thus far, my lord?"

"I shall leave that determination to my critics, madam." His brown eyes met hers. "I do think *Valiant Lady* a tolerable good play, but hardly a masterpiece."

"Indeed, sir?" said Verity, arching her dark eyebrows slightly.

A smile appeared on Ranley's lips as his eyes met Verity's. Before he could say anything further, one of the adoring throng diverted his attention. Dorchester had by this time come alongside his fiancée. Firmly grasping her by the arm, he pulled her away from the group. "Really, Verity, I will not tolerate you joining the fellow's featherheaded hangers-on."

Indignantly pulling her arm from Dorchester's grasp, Verity started to make an angry retort. However, her mother and aunt appeared beside them. "Ranley is such a clever man, is he not?" said Sarah, eyeing her famous guest with admiration. "How very fortunate he could be here. I do hope that he will do a recitation for us. That would be so very thrilling, would it not, Lord Dorchester?"

The marquess frowned, but managed a civil reply. "I should fancy the ladies would enjoy it."

"Oh, yes," said Lady Benbrook. "I do hope you will be able to persuade him, Sarah."

"I shall try," replied the marquise. "My dear guests," she said in a loud voice to command everyone's attention. "We will have some entertainment. I pray you will take a seat. Mrs. Bromley will favor us with a selection on the pianoforte and then Señor Velasquez will sing for us. Come, everyone, do sit down.''

Although the many guests surrounding Ranley looked disappointed, the baron himself seemed quite happy to have an excuse to break away. He quickly did as his hostess desired, taking a seat in one of the armchairs arranged in a concert-like fashion in the drawing room. Like a game of musical chairs, there was a rush to sit beside him and several ladies nearly collided trying to obtain one of the favored seats near Ranley. Verity had observed this unseemly haste among the ladies and was very much amused. She briefly caught the baron's eye as she passed serenely by him, casting an ironical gaze at him and raising her eyebrows once more.

Ranley was slightly irritated by Verity's amused glance. She was hoping to vex him, he thought, looking straight ahead. He knew that she had taken a seat somewhere behind him. He had an urge to turn and look at her, but restrained himself. Instead, he directed his attention to the woman in the seat beside him. That fortunate matron began chattering away, thrilled at her enviable position beside the eminent Lord Ranley.

Fortunately for the baron, the entertainment began and he was spared the necessity of making further conversation with the enthusiastic lady sitting beside him. The pianist was quite competent, skillfully playing a Mozart sonata. Her efforts were greeted enthusiastically by the assembled guests. As she began a second piece, Ranley found his mind wandering. He wondered if Lady Verity de Lacy was continuing to regard him with that ironical expression of hers. What rotten luck that she was there, he thought. He turned his head slightly, hoping to get a glimpse of her. Looking in the other direction, he finally spotted her, but found that she was not looking at him. She was staring at the pianist, apparently lost in the music.

Ranley was a little irritated with himself. Had he expected to find her gazing at him like a mooncalf? It was apparent what the young lady thought of him. When Mrs. Bromley finished her display of musical prowess, she stood and accepted the applause of the company with charming modesty.

She was followed by Señor Velazquez, a Spanish tenor of some reputation, who treated the audience to a number of stirring and, to Ranley, seemingly endless, operatic selections. The baron was quite pleased when Señor Velazquez completed his last aria and took his bows.

The Marquise de Chamfort rose and warmly praised both her musical guests. "Yes, how fortunate we are to have such artists among us. I know this is very bad of me, but I am hoping we can persuade one of our other guests to favor us with a selection. Lord Ranley, do say you will recite something for us."

The other guests burst into applause and cries of "Oh, do so, Lord Ranley."

The baron stood up and put up his hands to silence his admirers. "You are very kind," he said. "But it has been a very long time since I have faced an audience. I am grateful to Madame de Chamfort, but I beg you to allow me to decline this invitation. No, I could not do justice to the fine performances that have just taken place." The pronouncement was greeted by loud protests from the group. Ranley appeared flattered but unmoved by the pleas of the eager guests. "No, I have nothing prepared. Indeed, I would not know what to do."

"But I have a wonderful idea," cried Verity's aunt. "You could to a scene from *Romeo and Juliet* with my niece, Lady Verity de Lacy. She has the part memorized."

Verity, who had been enjoying herself immensely up to this point, looked horrified. The others applauded wildly and called her name. "Aunt," she cried, "you cannot be serious."

The marquise only smiled at Verity's dismay. She turned to the baron. "Lord Ranley, my niece is a wonderful Juliet. She has known the part since girlhood. Yes, this is a splendid idea!"

Ranley looked over at Verity and had the satisfaction of seeing her turn red with embarrassment. Despite his aversion to performing before the group, he could not resist the opportunity to disconcert the aggravating Lady Verity. "Why, yes, that is a good idea, Lady de Chamfort. Of course, perhaps Lady Verity has forgotten what she knew of the part."

Meeting Ranley's gaze, Verity frowned. There was a slight smile on his face and she knew that he was enjoying her discomfiture. "I have forgotten nothing," she said.

"Splendid," returned Ranley. "Then if the audience will still insist upon my making an exhibition of myself, I shall be happy to oblige."

The guests clapped delightedly and Verity rose from her chair. Dorchester, who was sitting beside her, looked horrified. "Verity, you cannot meant to . . ."

Verity ignored her fiancé and made her way to the front of the chairs to join the baron. Their eyes met and he smiled an irritating, mocking smile. Verity smiled in return. "The balcony scene, Lady Verity?" said Ranley.

"Indeed, what else?" replied Verity.

Ranley smiled broadly for a moment. Then, turning to the audience, he began. "But soft! what light through yonder window breaks? It is the east, and Juliet is the sun." Like everyone else in the room, Verity found herself riveted by the baron's words. His famous voice spoke the well-known lines with such compelling intensity that she was taken aback. Ranley continued to speak, thrilling his listeners with his speech.

Despite her embarrassment and confusion, Verity knew Juliet's role so well that she had no trouble saying her lines. "O Romeo, Romeo! Wherefore art thou Romeo? Deny thy father and refuse thy name; Or if thou wilt not, be but sworn my love, And I'll no longer be a Capulet." As she spoke, Ranley regarded her in some surprise. She's damned good, he told himself. He regarded her intently as she continued. "What's in a name? That which we call a rose By any other

name would smell as sweet. So Romeo would, were he not
Romeo call'd, Retain that dear perfection which he owes
Without that title. Romeo, doff they name, And for thy name,
which is no part of thee, Take all myself.''

Ranley looked into Verity's blue eyes. ''I take thee at thy
word. Call me but love and I'll be new baptiz'd. Henceforth
I never will be Romeo.''

Meeting his gaze, Verity found herself suddenly unaware
of the audience. She saw only Ranley, who was regarding
her with the passionate intensity of a devoted Romeo. They
continued with the scene, much to the delight of the
assembled guests, who were decidedly disappointed when
it concluded.

''Good night, good night!'' said Ranley, eyeing Verity with
an expression that made several female onlookers feel like
swooning. ''Parting is such sweet sorrow, that I shall say
good night till it be morrow.''

The audience stared in rapt silence for a moment and then
broke into long enthusiastic applause and shouts of approval.
The loud noise brought both Ranley and Verity back to
reality. He looked at her and smiled. He bowed first to the
audience and then to her in obvious tribute. Fearing she was
blushing, Verity smiled and tried to appear calm. In truth,
it had been a most unsettling experience.

''More, more!'' cried some of the gentlemen in the crowd,
but Ranley put up his hand to silence them.

''You are so very kind,'' he said, ''but Lady Verity and
I have done our duty.'' They were applauded once again and
then everyone rose from their chairs to surround them and
declare that never before had anyone seen a better rendition
of the famous scene than they had witnessed that evening.

Dorchester stood aside staring sullenly. He had not been
at all pleased at Verity's performance. He thought it was quite
unseemly for her to have made a spectacle of herself, taking
the part of a common actress. The way she had looked at
Ranley there before all the company was unspeakably

improper. Why, one might have thought there was something between them, thought the marquess disgustedly.

Dorchester frowned as he looked at Verity accept the accolades of her aunt's guests. She had always been wild and unconcerned about what people thought of her. Perhaps he was foolish thinking he could keep her in check once they were married. Perhaps he should have chosen another more suitable girl, someone more easily managed.

"What is the matter, Dorchester?" said a gentleman coming up beside the marquess. "You look positively blue-deviled."

Dorchester looked over at the newcomer, whom he recognized as an acquaintance of his, Charles Allenby. "Allenby," said the marquess, acknowledging the other gentleman's presence.

Allenby fixed his bejeweled quizzing glass upon Verity. "By God, you are a lucky man, my lord, to be marrying such a lovely lady. And what a stirring performance. By my faith, I was nearly moved to tears."

Frowning, Dorchester fixed an icy look upon Allenby. "Your pardon, sir, but I must join Lady Verity."

As the marquess moved away, Allenby smiled delightedly. It was a very interesting evening, he reflected. He had told numerous friends that he had seen Verity de Lacy and Ranley in a carriage together and the story had been dismissed as a mistake or fabrication. Seeing the way Ranley and Verity looked at each other gave credence to the tale. Indeed, thought Allenby, if the two were not already lovers, it would not be long before they were. Looking smug, Allenby went off to find a more congenial companion.

11

Lord Ranley drove his stylish curricle through the busy traffic toward the Queen's Theater. His lordship was in a particularly good mood that afternoon, so good that he did not even curse a careless wagon driver who pulled his lumbering vehicle into the path of his horses, forcing the baron into quick evasive action.

Ranley was not aware of the cause of his good temper although he suspected that the fine May sunshine contributed to his unusual feeling of well-being. Whatever the explanation, the baron had somehow shaken off the gloom and indifference that had plagued him for many weeks.

That morning he had risen early and, foregoing his usual fortification of liquor, he had begun work on a play. He had written a number of pages and had been not displeased with the result.

When he arrived at the theater, the baron issued a cheery greeting to the ever-present Jenkins. He then proceeded to Hawkins's office where he found his friend at his desk immersed in a veritable sea of paper.

"Good day to you, Billy," said Ranley, entering the office and pulling up a chair near Hawkins's desk.

"Brutus," returned the theater manager. "You appear dashed chipper. If you had my bills to pay, you'd not be so cheerful."

"So you pay your bills, do you, Billy? I can recall many a week that I waited for my wages."

Hawkins grinned. "Aye, but there was many a week when I had not two pennies to rub together. We were not always so prosperous, my lad."

"That is a fact of which I am well aware, Billy." Ranley smiled. "But the times we had."

"Aye, we had many a good time in those days," returned Hawkins. He paused and eyed his friend curiously. "You are in a good mood today. You must have won at cards last night."

Ranley smiled again. "I never win at cards, Billy."

"Well, I know that, my lad. You are hopeless as a gamester. That is why I am always telling you to take care or you'll lose that fine fortune of yours."

"There is no need to preach to me, Billy. I am taking your advice and avoiding the gaming tables."

"You are?" said Hawkins, quite astonished. "Well, I'm damned, but glad am I to hear it."

"Yes, I spent last evening in the most harmless way, attending a soiree at the home of the Marquise de Chamfort. I behaved myself, Billy. I drank only two glasses of the lady's excellent champagne and performed like a trained bear for the company."

"Performed?"

Ranley nodded. "I played Romeo to Lady Verity de Lacy's Juliet."

"Lady Verity de Lacy? Good God, was she there?"

"Don't look so horrified, Billy. And, although this will surprise you, I can say that she was the best Juliet I have ever seen."

"It does not surprise me," muttered Hawkins. "The girl is a clever minx, too clever by half by my way of thinking."

"You should have seen her, Billy. What an actress she would make. And she is damnably attractive."

Hawkins viewed his friend in some alarm. "Good God, Brutus, you talk as if you are in love with the chit."

"Don't be absurd, Billy," replied the baron. "I have no intention of falling in love with her or with anyone."

"A man never intends to fall in love," returned the older man. "It just happens like a toothache."

Ranley laughed. "What a romantic you are, Billy."

"I only believe in keeping my wits about me. This Lady Verity may try to ensnare you. You had best be wary. There is many a female who would wish to find herself Lady Ranley."

"My dear Billy, I doubt that Lady Verity is one of them. And if she is trying to ensnare me, she is going about it in a very odd way. Why, last evening she delighted in making me feel a fool. After all, I am the man who was so easily bamboozled into thinking I had written a play while drunk."

"Most playwrights write their plays while drunk," said Hawkins. "It is not so unusual."

Ranley grinned. "I still have not forgiven you for hoodwinking me, Billy. I do hope you have sent Lady Verity her payment for the play."

Hawkins hesitated. "I believe I have done so, Brutus, but as you can see, there are so many details I must attend to."

"You bounder. You have not sent her the hundred pounds, have you?"

"It is not that I do not intend to do so, but it is only that I have not had opportunity to see to my accounts."

Ranley frowned ominously. "You will pay the lady and you will do so today. Is that understood, Billy?"

"Very well, Brutus. I shall do so this very day."

"Do I have your word on that?"

"My solemn oath," said Hawkins earnestly.

"Good. Now I wanted to tell you that I am writing a new play. It's a comedy."

"A comedy? That is splendid, Brutus."

"I think it will be good." He paused and smiled. "Though I daresay it will not be as good as my last play, *Valiant Lady.*"

Hawkins laughed, happy that Ranley seemed able to joke about the matter. "I have an idea, Brutus. Let us go to the Crown and Anchor. I've need of sustenance and it would be like old times."

Ranley nodded, pleased at the idea of visiting the public house he had long abandoned. Happy with his young friend's good humor, Hawkins merrily accompanied the baron from the office.

Verity looked down at her paper and frowned. She was having some difficulty concentrating on her work, a fact that annoyed her very much. Verity was worried that her new play was not going very well. Of course, she had little time to write, for the busy social season consisted of endless engagements, most of them late-night affairs that caused one to sleep the morning away. Afternoons were spent either making calls or receiving them or discussing menus or gowns.

This particular afternoon was free only because Lady Benbrook felt very tired and needed a nap in preparation for the evening's dinner party. Verity had been pleased to find she had a few hours to herself, but soon she was despairing that she did not feel at all like writing. Every time she tried to put down something on the paper, her mind would wander and she would find herself daydreaming. To her considerable irritation, the object of her reflections was the aggravating Lord Ranley.

Try as she might, Verity could not keep from thinking about the handsome baron. She kept hearing the melodious tones of his voice reciting Romeo's lines. It was positively irksome, thought Verity, to think of the man. After all, she was no silly schoolgirl and she was hardly prone to ridiculous infatuations. No, indeed, she was a young woman of two and twenty and a professional authoress who had recently sold a play for the considerable sum of one hundred pounds.

The thought of the money Hawkins had promised succeeded in driving Ranley from her mind. It had been three weeks since the theater manager had agreed to pay her for the play. After waiting a fortnight, Verity had written him a polite letter reminding him of his obligation. As of yet, there had been no reply.

"Nell!" cried Verity suddenly. "Nell, do come here!"

Nell, who had been straightening things in Verity's wardrobe, came quickly. "What is it, my lady?"

"I have been thinking of that rogue Hawkins. He said he would pay me one hundred pounds. He has not done so. I am beginning to think that he has no intention of doing so."

"Do you think he is dishonest, my lady?"

"I know that he is dishonest, Nell. Stealing my play was the act of a blackguard."

"Surely Lord Ranley will see that your ladyship receives the money."

"I scarcely think Lord Ranley gives me a thought, Nell," returned Verity ill-humoredly. "I have been thinking, Nell." The servant noted Verity's expression and braced herself. "I have been thinking that if I wish to obtain this money due me, I must go get it myself. You and I will go to the Queen's Theater and see Mr. Hawkins."

"Are you sure that is a wise idea, my lady?"

Verity smiled. "I do not care if it is wise or not, Nell. It is what I have decided."

"Very well, my lady."

"So fetch my bonnet, my dear Nell, and yours as well."

"Yes, my lady."

"And tell Weeks to have the carriage brought 'round. Have him inform my mother we have gone to the milliner's."

Nell nodded and hastened to obey her instructions. She was reminded of the other similar excursion they had made, calling on Lord Ranley. Still, that had not turned out so badly. She had been able to ride in a carriage with the famous playwright and her mistress had become one hundred pounds richer. One hundred pounds. Nell could hardly imagine such a princely sum. No wonder Lady Verity was so vexed for not receiving it. As Nell hurried down the stairs she devoutly hoped that Mr. Hawkins would pay what he had promised. A slight smile crossed Nell's face. Woe to him if he did not, she thought, and then went to find Weeks, the butler.

The ride to the Queen's Theater did not take long. Soon Nell Dawson found herself following her determined mistress into the august theatrical establishment. The watchful Jenkins greeted Verity with a bow and inquired how he might assist her. "I should like to see Mr. Hawkins."

"I am sorry, miss," replied Jenkins. "Mr. Hawkins is not at the theater at present."

"Indeed," replied Verity, looking very unhappy at the news. "Would you know where he might be?"

Jenkins rubbed his chin. "He has gone to the Crown and Anchor. 'Tis a public house. They set a very respectable table there, miss."

"And where is the Crown and Anchor?"

"Oh, it is not very far, miss. Just go two blocks down that way," he said, pointing, "and turn to the right. You'll not miss the sign."

"Thank you," said Verity. "Come along, Nell."

After being assisted back into the carriage by the groom, Verity ordered the driver to the Crown and Anchor. In a few moments they were there. "We won't be very long, Stewart," said Verity, addressing the driver.

The servant eyed the pub with disapproval. Long in the earl's employ, Stewart did not think the Crown and Anchor the sort of place Lady Verity should be visiting. "If your ladyship be wanting to go in there, I or Harry will accompany you."

"Don't be silly, Stewart. I shall come to no harm inside."

"But, my lady . . ."

"No, Stewart, I shall not need you. I shall not be long. You wait here. Harry may wait near the door if it will make you feel better."

"It will indeed, my lady," replied Stewart. Harry jumped down and hurried to assist the young women from the vehicle. He then followed them inside. Stewart sat waiting in the carriage, very much relieved that Harry was with his mistress. Harry was a brawny youth well able to protect the young ladies. As he took out his pipe, Stewart reflected that he did not much like driving Lady Verity to theaters and public houses. The earl would have his hide if he knew about it. He wondered what business his young lady could possibly have at the Crown and Anchor. Lighting his pipe, Stewart shrugged and continued waiting.

The Crown and Anchor was a lively establishment favored by actors and denizens of the theater. Evenings it was often filled with a raucous crowd, eating and drinking and enjoying themselves in a noisy, rowdy fashion. That afternoon, however, it was a fairly quiet place, filled with hungry patrons partaking of the Crown and Anchor's excellent mutton and kidney pie.

Verity looked around for Hawkins, but could not find him. The publican, seeing the unaccustomed sight of a lady of quality entering his establishment, came forward. "Might I help you, madam?"

Verity smiled graciously. "You are very good, sir. I am seeking Mr. Hawkins of the Queen's Theater."

"He is here, madam. Do follow me and I shall take you to him."

Verity nodded and then she and Nell followed the man past a number of tables. Suddenly Verity spied Hawkins seated at a table in the far corner of the public house. He was talking loudly to a companion whose back was to her. "There is Mr. Hawkins, ma'am."

"Thank you." Verity and Nell approached the table and

it was only when they were very close that Verity recognized the gentleman seated across from Hawkins. It was Baron Ranley.

Hawkins saw the two young ladies and looked startled. "Good heavens," he said. "You ladies here?"

Ranley turned in their direction and rose quickly to his feet. "My lady Juliet and Miss Dawson," he said. "What an unexpected pleasure."

"Lord Ranley," said Verity, hoping she sounded convincingly indifferent to the dashing baron's presence. "I have come to see Mr. Hawkins. I went to the theater, but I was told I might find you here."

"What a great honor, my lady," said Hawkins, who having risen from his seat, bowed with a flourish. "Do sit down, ladies."

Nell looked at her mistress uncertainly, but Verity smiled and sat down at the table, assisted by Lord Ranley. Hawkins gallantly helped Nell with her chair. "I shall be brief, Mr. Hawkins," said Verity. "I have not received the compensation due me. That is why I have come to see you. I believe you have had sufficient time to send me the money."

"Indeed he has," said Ranley, directing a warning look at Hawkins. "Billy, you will pay her ladyship immediately or you will answer to me."

"My dear young lady," said Hawkins, ignoring the baron, "you must understand that one does not have such large sums of money at one's fingertips. No, indeed. I am not a rich man."

"You are a damnable miser, Billy," said Ranley. He looked at Verity. "Do not fear, Lady Verity, you will have your hundred pounds. We will go to the Queen's Theater where I will force this pennypinching rapscallion to pay you."

"Thank you, Lord Ranley," said Verity. "I suppose you must think me a bold, avaricious person." She smiled. "In truth, I suppose I am."

Ranley burst into laughter at this pronouncement. "You are no match for this formidable lady, Billy."

"I daresay I am not," said Hawkins, reconciling himself to parting with the one hundred pounds. "But now that the business is over, would you ladies care for something to eat or drink?"

"That is very good of you," said Verity, "but no."

"Come then, Billy, let us escort the ladies back to the theater."

"Very well," replied Hawkins taking a last swig from his mug of ale.

Just as they were about to rise from the table, a commanding feminine voice called out. "My dear Brutus and Mr. Hawkins!"

The baron looked over to see the queenly form of Mrs. Fleming approach the table. She was accompanied by a stout red-haired gentleman. Ranley and Hawkins rose politely. "Maria," said his lordship.

"How lucky to find you here. Do allow us to join you." Without waiting for a reply, Mrs. Fleming took a seat next to Verity. She smiled serenely at the young ladies and then looked expectantly at Ranley.

"Oh, yes," said the baron, "introductions are in order. Mrs. Fleming, may I present Lady Verity de Lacy and Miss Dawson? Ladies, may I present Mrs. Fleming and Mr. Fleming?"

"Mrs. Fleming needs no introduction," said Verity, extending her hand. "I am a great admirer of yours, ma'am."

"How kind, Lady Verity," returned the actress, very much delighted at Verity's civility. Mrs. Fleming's profession as well as her humble origins severely limited her acquaintance with titled ladies. Yet the scorn with which most of the women of the first circles of society regarded her only made Mrs. Fleming want desperately to be accepted by them. She knew all about the first families of the kingdom and knew very well that the de Lacy name was one of the most ancient and respected names in England.

She also knew that Verity was engaged to marry the Marquess of Dorchester and that she would one day be a duchess. For Maria Fleming, the idea of being on friendly terms with a future duchess was irresistable.

"I saw you in *Valiant Lady*," said Verity, genuinely thrilled at meeting the famous actress. "It was a very moving performance."

"A compliment from you is a compliment indeed, my lady," said Mrs. Fleming, smiling broadly. "I do adore the play. I have never so loved a role as that of Princess Flavia." She smiled at Ranley. "I must say his lordship did himself proud with such a brilliant tragedy."

"Yes," said Verity, looking over at the baron. "You are so very discerning, Mrs. Fleming. He most certainly did."

"It is his best work," continued the actress, "although I should not wish to puff him up like a peacock."

Verity nearly laughed, but restrained herself. She looked over at Ranley and smiled mischievously at him. The baron arched his dark eyebrows slightly and smiled in return.

12

Maria Fleming could scarcely believe her good fortune in having met Lady Verity that afternoon. Maria had been very pleased that the young lady had been so amiable, totally lacking the haughty condescension one might have expected from one of her rank.

While applying her theatrical makeup and donning her costume that evening, Maria told everyone within hearing about her new acquaintance with Lady Verity. All of her colleagues seemed properly impressed that the aristocratic young lady had had such a high opinion of Maria's accomplishments.

Buoyed by her fellow actors' admiration and her own high spirits, Maria outdid herself that evening, playing Princess Flavia with such abandon that the crowd roared its approval. After the performance, Maria curtsied time and time again while her devotees cheered and tossed flowers onto the stage.

It had been a wildly successful evening, thought Maria as she removed her makeup and changed into a peach-colored evening dress. Her current beau, a young dandy named Sir

Arthur Cavendish, arrived at the dressing room door to escort her to the Crown and Anchor where a boisterous group of actors and theatergoers were now gathering.

When she arrived at the public house, Maria was greeted with enthusiastic cheers, which she received with a gracious nod and a regal wave of her hand. Sir Arthur led Maria through the admiring throng to a table where a group of noisy revelers was assembled. Seated there were theater manager Hawkins, Lord Ranley, Andrew Drummond, who was Maria's leading man, and two of the supporting actresses. All of them looked particularly cheerful as they downed flagons of ale.

Maria fixed her gaze upon Ranley and smiled, much to the disapproval of her escort. "I had hoped you would be here, Brutus. Were you at the theater?"

"Regrettably, no," said Ranley. "Billy has told me that you were a triumph, Maria." He raised his mug. "I salute you, fair princess."

"Hear, hear," said the others, toasting the leading lady and gulping down the Crown and Anchor's heady brew.

"But sit down, both of you," said Hawkins. "What a glorious night for the Queen's Theater."

"Indeed so," said Andrew Drummond, his speech slightly slurred. "A glorious night."

Maria directed Sir Arthur to fetch her a chair, and place it next to Ranley. A rather disgruntled Sir Arthur then found himself a seat on the other side of the table where he closely watched his lady love and the insufferably handsome Lord Ranley.

Hawkins called to a barmaid to bring more ale for the new arrivals and soon everyone was talking loudly and laughing at what so easily passed for witticisms among such inebriated company. The baron, although showing unusual forbearance in his consumption of alcohol, was enjoying himself. As he sat there with his fellow thespians, he realized how much he had missed his colleagues. The sporting gentlemen with whom he had of late been spending most of his time were poor substitutes for such jovial companions. It felt good to be back there among them all.

"I wish you had seen the play," said Maria.

"So do I," replied Ranley, taking a sip of his ale.

"I have never had such a fine evening. And this afternoon meeting you and Lady—"

Ranley cut her off. "My dear Maria, I think it best not to bandy the young lady's name about."

"Oh, yes," said Maria.

"Bandy about what young lady's name?" said Andrew Drummond.

"Nothing of any concern to you, Mr. Drummond," said Maria severely.

"Oh," returned Drummond, who shrugged and then turned his attention back to his drinking.

"I did not know you would not want me to talk about meeting her," said Maria, leaning toward the baron and speaking with a low voice. She looked thoughtful for a moment and then frowned. "What was she doing here with you and Billy? Brutus, you scoundrel!"

"My dear Maria, you have drawn the wrong conclusion."

"And what, pray, is the proper conclusion to be drawn?"

Ranley paused, unsure how to reply. "The lady thinks herself a playwright," he said finally. "She had sent a play for Billy and me to read."

"Oh," said Maria, very much relieved. "Did you read it?"

"Yes," said Hawkins, entering the conversation. "Dreadful stuff it was. Had to let the lass down gently."

"Yes, Billy was the very essence of tact and kindliness," said Ranley, directing an ironical gaze at his friend.

"Well, I am glad to find that you had no improper intentions toward such a fine young lady, Brutus," said Maria.

"Maria, you can scarcely conclude that about his lordship's intentions," said Hawkins with a grin. "But as I was there to keep him in check, there was no threat to the lady's virtue.''

The famed actress eyed both Hawkins and Ranley with a trace of suspicion. ''Did you not think her very pretty, Brutus?''

''She was not ill-favored,'' said the baron nonchalantly.

''Well, you are a very poor judge if you did not think her very pretty indeed, Brutus.''

''Perhaps it was only that she was so overshadowed by your own beauty, my dear Maria,'' replied Brutus with his famous smile.

Although pronouncing it outrageous flummery, Maria smiled at the compliment and allowed herself to be diverted from the topic of Lady Verity de Lacy.

The following day Verity rose early in the morning and went to her desk. There she unlocked the secret drawer and took out a leather purse containing one hundred pounds in gold.

Nell Dawson entered the room and shook her head at her mistress. ''My lady, you must not be taking that from the drawer. What if someone should see you?''

''I can't help it,'' said Verity, untying the strings of the purse and pouring the shiny coins into her lap.

''What will you do with the money, my lady?''

''I don't know,'' returned Verity, putting the coins back into the pouch. ''I shall hide it away like a squirrel with a prized acorn, Nell. Why, I feel like a proper miser.'' She secreted the money in the drawer and locked it. ''I daresay Hawkins would never have given it to me if Ranley had not been there. I expect I must be grateful to him.''

Nell suppressed a sigh. ''Truly, my lady, is not Lord Ranley a dashing gentleman? I nearly thought I should swoon sitting so near to him.''

''Good heavens, Nell, do cease talking like a simpleton. Come, I must get dressed. We will take a walk in the park.''

Nodding, Nell hurried to fetch appropriate attire for such

an excursion. She was very happy at the idea for Nell loved strolling about the streets of London. There was always so much to see and so many interesting people about.

The dog Jackanapes somehow seemed to know Verity's plans and he hurried up to them as they approached the front door. "Oh, Jack, why don't you wait for Mama?" said Verity. The little dog only cocked his head and grinned expectantly. "Oh, very well, you may go." Jackanapes let out a high-pitched yip of excitement as Nell went to get his leash.

Soon Verity, Nell, and their frisky companion were on their way to the park. It was early, too early for most of the fashionable set to have made their appearance. Verity loved this time of day and she was most appreciative of the excellent June weather.

"It was very exciting meeting Mrs. Fleming," said Nell.

"Oh, yes," said Verity. "Oh, I know I was not altogether pleased at how she played Princess Thalia—or, I should say Princess Flavia—but one must concede she is a personage of considerable consequence."

"And she is beautiful."

"Indeed, yes," said Verity.

"Do you think she is in love with Lord Ranley, my lady?"

Verity turned to her maid with a look of annoyance. "Whyever would you think so?"

"Well, Antoinette said that they were once . . ." She stopped in midsentence.

"Were once what, Nell?"

Nell hesitated, wondering how to phrase her reply with suitable delicacy.

"You mean they were lovers, Nell?"

"My lady!" said Nell, blushing. "Yes, that is what I mean."

"It is a matter of complete indifference to me," said Verity. "And I suggest you refrain from repeating such gossip to me heard below stairs."

"Yes, my lady," replied Nell meekly.

Verity burst into laughter. "Nell Dawson, what a goose you are. If you do not repeat gossip to me, I shall never forgive you. You know I adore gossip."

They both laughed and continued on. Arriving at the park, they walked briskly inside with the dog Jackanapes running alongside Verity and pulling on his leash.

"My lady!" cried Nell suddenly. "Is that not Lord Ranley?"

"Ranley here?" said Verity. She looked in the direction her maid was staring. It was Ranley. Mounted on a tall chestnut horse, the baron rode alone. He looked undeniably handsome seated atop the splendid animal, although Verity noted that he had the look of an unpracticed rider and seemed to be a trifle uncomfortable with the spirited horse beneath him.

Verity watched him with interest, thinking that he would not see them. However, Ranley turned his head in their direction and spotted them immediately. He pulled his horse up short and then rode toward them.

"He is coming this way," cried Nell. "Oh, my lady, what if I do swoon?"

"Oh, Nell!"

"Good morning, ladies." Doffing his hat, the baron smiled his most charming smile down at them.

"Good morning, Lord Ranley," said Verity.

"Good morning, my lord," said Nell, who appeared in no danger of swooning now that Ranley was before them.

Whether Jackanapes took a dislike to the baron or to his horse, the little dog was apparently unhappy with the newcomers. He barked and then bared his teeth in a growl. The chestnut horse shied a bit, but Ranley controlled it with some difficulty.

"I did not expect to see you here, Lord Ranley," said Verity, pulling Jackanapes in closer to her side.

"Nor did I, Lady Verity," returned the baron. "I do not often rise so early and go riding. I'm damned if I know why I yielded to such an urge this morning."

"Perhaps the lovely weather," suggested Verity.

"Perhaps," said Ranley, noting that Verity looked quite stunning in her simple white walking dress and straw bonnet. She has the most damnably blue eyes, thought the baron.

"I am glad to have the opportunity to thank you, my lord," said Verity, "for forcing Mr. Hawkins to pay me."

"He is a tight-fisted old curmudgeon," said Ranley with a smile, "but he is a good fellow nonetheless. I daresay it was little enough he could pay for my greatest play."

Verity smiled and was about to reply when Jackanapes pulled at his leash and lunged suddenly at the horse's back legs. The frightened creature kicked wildly and then reared up on its hind legs, depositing a startled baron onto the ground with a thud.

"Jack!" cried Verity, yanking hard on his leash. The little dog barked noisily and the spooked horse made a dash for the opposite end of the park. "Oh, Ranley, are you hurt?"

The baron shook his head. "It is only my dignity that has suffered." He started to get to his feet, but as he put his weight on his ankle, he winced in pain.

"You are hurt!" cried Verity, rushing to his side and helping him to stand.

Ranley moved his hessian-clad foot gingerly. "It is nothing serious."

"Your horse, my lord," said Nell. "We'll not be able to catch him."

"He is a hired mount and he is doubtless heading back to the stables to complain to his fellows of his ill treatment," said Ranley.

Verity looked around the park. She had never seen it so empty. There was no one about to assist Ranley. "Can you walk, sir?" said Verity.

"Yes, I'm certain of it," said the baron, taking a tentative step.

"My house is very close," said Verity. "We will go there and then Stewart will take you in the carriage."

"I shall be most happy to take advantage of your kind suggestion, Lady Verity." He looked down at Jackanapes, who was snapping at him. "Be quiet, you little fiend," he growled. "See what you have done, you mouse-sized hound of Hell."

Quelled by the baron's words, the dog appeared contrite. Verity laughed. "You are a monster, Jack. Come, Lord Ranley, I shall take your arm and Nell your other arm. We'll get you back to the house."

"I confess I do like the arrangement," said the baron as the young ladies took their positions. "I come with a broken-down hack of a horse and leave with two pretty girls."

"That was hardly a broken-down hack, sir," said Verity as they walked slowly toward the entrance to the park. "He was a fine-looking horse."

"You see, I know so little about the creatures, I do not know the difference. I daresay this is damned embarrassing. You probably think me a poor horseman indeed, Lady Verity."

"I would not say that, my lord."

"But you undoubtedly think so."

"It is not easy to control a spooked mount," said Verity. "Even an experienced horseman cannot always do so."

"And you do not consider me an experienced horseman, my lady?"

"Shall we say that I suggest your lordship not attempt steeplechasing very soon?" Verity rather regretted her joke, but Ranley burst into laughter and she and Nell joined in.

In a short time they were at Benbrook house and a watchful footman was hurrying to their aid. "Really, I am quite fine, Lady Verity."

Verity ignored him. "Tom, do help Lord Ranley into the drawing room and have Stewart bring the carriage to take him home."

"Aye, m'lady," said Tom, hurrying to help the baron up the steps to the front door. Soon Ranley was safely ensconced on one of the sofas in the drawing room.

After placing the troublesome lapdog into the care of Weeks, the butler, Verity, followed by Nell, joined the baron. "I am so sorry this happened. It was Jackanapes's fault. Shall I have Tom fetch the physician?"

"By all the gods, no, Lady Verity," said Ranley. "I am barely hurt. It is a slight sprain. It seems better already."

"What has happened?" Verity turned in surprise to see her father standing in the doorway. Although the earl seldom rose before eleven and it was scarcely nine o'clock, there he was dressed and ready for the day.

"Papa," said Verity. "This is Lord Ranley. He has had a slight mishap in the park and has injured his ankle. Lord Ranley, may I present my father, Lord Benbrook."

The baron got unsteadily to his feet despite Verity's protests. "Your servant, Lord Benbrook."

"Do sit down, sir," said Benbrook. "Don't be a fool to stand on a bad leg."

Ranley sat down again. "Lady Verity makes too much of my injury. It is nothing, I assure you."

"We met Lord Ranley in the park, Papa," said Verity. "Jackanapes lunged toward his horse and the animal reared unexpectedly."

"Indeed?" said Benbrook with a frown.

"I have asked Stewart to bring 'round the carriage to take Lord Ranley home, Papa."

"Lady Verity has been most kind," said Ranley.

"But whatever are you doing up so early, Papa?" said Verity.

"I was going riding with Dorchester," said the earl.

"Dorchester?" said Verity.

"He should be here any minute." Scarcely had the earl said these words when the butler appeared to announce the Marquess of Dorchester. The gentleman entered the room attired in an olive-green coat, buff riding breeches, and dazzling hessian boots with gold tassels. He regarded Ranley in mute astonishment.

"I daresay you have not met Ranley," said Benbrook.

"Indeed, I have not," returned Dorchester, eyeing the baron with disfavor.

Ranley did not attempt to get to his feet. "You must excuse me, my lord," he said. "Sprained my ankle."

Dorchester bowed stiffly to the baron and then looked at Verity. "Good morning, Gerald," she said. "We met Lord Ranley in the park. The poor man was thrown from his horse. It was all my fault, or I should say it was the fault of Jackanapes, but then I was responsible for him so it was my fault."

"I trust you are not badly hurt, Ranley," said Dorchester.

"Not at all. It was not serious."

Weeks appeared in the doorway. "The carriage is ready, my lord."

"Then my man will take you home, Ranley," said Benbrook.

"That is very kind of you, Lord Benbrook," said the baron, rising to his feet. "And my thanks to you, Lady Verity, and to Miss Dawson."

As he said these words, Ranley looked directly into Verity's eyes, and she was momentarily disconcerted. "It was nothing, sir. I am sorry that it happened."

Smiling, Ranley considered that he was not all that sorry it happened. In fact, he had very much enjoyed leaning on Lady Verity's arm. "Thank you again," he said as Tom and Weeks assisted him from the drawing room. Nell then took her leave, quickly vanishing from sight.

When Ranley was safely gone, Dorchester folded his arms across his chest and frowned. "Good heavens, Verity, what possessed you to bring the man back here?"

"What else could I do, Gerald? His horse had run away. He could not walk very far and no one else was about."

"The man is notorious, Verity," said Dorchester testily. "You should not be civil to him."

"Come, come, Dorchester," said the earl. "Verity could do nothing but what she did. There was no harm in it. But

I do not like the idea of admitting a playactor to my house. Oh, yes, he is now a peer, but he made his living as a common actor. We should have nothing to do with a man like that.''

"Oh, Papa," Verity said. She would have protested, but Lady Benbrook appeared. The countess had risen upon learning of Ranley's arrival. She had hurriedly dressed and was obviously disappointed at finding that her famous guest had already departed.

"He has gone?" cried Lady Benbrook. "Oh, Benbrook, why did you not keep him longer?"

Verity looked at her father, and, seeing him frown, burst into laughter.

13

After breakfast the following day, Verity and her mother retreated to the drawing room where they sorted through the morning post. "Oh, look, my dear," said Lady Benbrook, after opening one of the numerous invitations that had arrived that day. "It is for the Princess de la Bretonne's ball."

"How exciting," said Verity, eagerly taking the invitation from her mother. "This is one one occasion I shall be very glad to attend. I have heard so much about the princess."

"I daresay everyone has heard about her. She is rather notorious, but she is a dear friend of your Aunt Sarah. It is Sarah who has secured us these invitations. I wrote to her requesting that she use her influence. This will doubtless be the most splendid affair of the Season. I do hope Sarah succeeded in obtaining invitations for the Haverfords and Dorchester."

"Oh, Mama," said Verity, "must you always bring Gerald into the conversation?"

"My dear girl, may I remind you that you are to wed the gentleman in scarce three weeks' time?"

Verity made no reply, but glanced back down at the invitation. "The ball is less than a fortnight away. I shall not yet be Lady Dorchester." She pronounced the name with a distasteful expression. "Lady Dorchester. Oh, Mama, I do not like the sound of it."

"You will grow accustomed to it, Verity," said the countess severely. "Now I do hope you do not intend to become difficult about your marriage. I did think you were behaving so well about it."

"No, Mama, I shall not be difficult. Let us speak no more of my wedding. Should we not see to the other letters and invitations?"

Lady Benbrook nodded. "Indeed we should, my dear," she said and took up another of the letters. "Here is a letter for you, Verity."

Verity took the missive from her mother and opened it. "It is from Lord Ranley."

"Lord Ranley?" exclaimed the countess. "What does it say?"

Verity read from the letter. " 'My Lady, I wish to thank you for your kindness to me after my unfortunate misadventure. Be assured that my injury was not serious and, if my esteemed leech is to be believed, I shall be recovered in a few days. Would that the injury to my dignity could be so easily healed. Praise God that I never claimed to be a horseman. Again, my thanks. Your obedient servant, Ranley.' "

"I do wish I had been there to see him," said Lady Benbrook, taking the letter and perusing it. "He is a charming man."

"Yes," said Verity absently.

"Your father was quite upset at having Ranley here. Indeed, he can be so unreasonable. If it were up to me, I should like to invite Ranley to dinner."

"Oh, Mama, would you?" said Verity.

"I should not dare," returned the countess. "Your father

would have my head. No, my dear, we have seen the last of Ranley.''

"Yes,'' replied Verity with a frown. "I suppose we have.'' She took back the letter from her mother and Lady Benbrook turned her attention to the rest of the correspondence.

That afternoon Verity sat in the library studying a rather ponderous volume of history. The house was quiet for the countess had retired to her room for a nap and the earl had left for his club.

After a time Verity closed the book and placed it back upon the shelf. She felt restless and preoccupied. Although she usually enjoyed reading history, she did not seem to be in the mood for any serious study.

Verity wondered if she should try to work on her new play, but decided against it. No, she would not be able to accomplish anything, she told herself. Every time she tried to concentrate on anything, her mind would wander and she would begin to think of Ranley. Since receiving his note that morning, she had scarcely been able to think of anything else. Sighing, Verity began to look about the library shelves for some other reading material, but she was interrupted by the appearance of the butler.

"I beg your pardon, my lady,'' said Weeks. "There are visitors. Shall I say your ladyship is not receiving?''

"Yes, Weeks.'' The butler bowed and began to leave. "Wait!''

"Yes, my lady?''

"Who is it, Weeks? Perhaps I will see the. I am in need of diversion.''

"It is a Mrs. Boyd and a Mrs. Fleming,'' said Weeks.

"Mrs. Fleming? The actress?''

"I venture to think so, my lady,'' returned the butler.

"Oh, this is excellent, Weeks. Do show them to the drawing room.''

Weeks looked a trifle surprised, but he only nodded and

left the library. When he informed the visitors that Lady Verity would see them, Maria directed a very well-satisfied look at her companion.

That lady, an attractive younger woman with blond hair and rouged cheeks, raised her eyebrows. After Weeks had ushered them into the drawing room, Mrs. Boyd shook her head. "I must say, Maria, I did not expect the likes of them that owns such a place as this would allow us across the doorstep."

"Did I not tell you Lady Verity was a very considerate young lady? She is also an admirer of my work."

Mrs. Boyd nodded, clearly impressed. She then looked about the drawing room, noting the costly furniture and works of art that decorated it. It was not long before Verity arrived. "Good afternoon, ladies. How good of you to call, Mrs. Fleming." The actress glowed at Verity's enthusiastic welcome, hoping that her friend would take note of it. "My mother is resting so she cannot join us." As she said these words, Verity suppressed a smile, knowing full well that Lady Benbrook would never have received the two women who stood before her.

"Lady Verity," said Maria, "may I present my dear friend, Mrs. Boyd? Mrs. Boyd, Lady Verity de Lacy."

"How do you do?" said Verity politely. "I am so very glad to meet you, Mrs. Boyd. If my memory serves, I saw you in the role of Jocasta in *Warrior*—that is to say, *Valiant Lady*. You were excellent. You were all excellent."

"You are kind, my lady," said Mrs. Boyd, beaming at the praise. "I cannot imagine how you remembered me. And to remember the name of the role I played. Why, your ladyship has a prodigious memory."

Verity smiled. "Oh, I assure you, it was not difficult for me. Do sit down, ladies. Would you care for tea?"

Maria exchanged a look with her companion. "That would be very nice, Lady Verity."

Verity nodded and rang for a servant. After instructions

were given for tea, she sat down with her guests. "I do appreciate having the opportunity to talk with you. I have a great interest in the theater."

"And I am told that your ladyship would make a fine actress," said Mrs. Boyd, "that is, if you were not a lady, of course."

Verity laughed. "And where did you hear such a thing, Mrs. Boyd?"

"From Lord Ranley. He said that you played Juliet ever so nicely and we girls should be glad you are not on the stage."

"He was exaggerating," said Verity, pleased to hear that Ranley had complimented her. "Do you ladies enjoy your work in the theater?"

Maria shrugged. "Oh, much of the time we do, Lady Verity, but 'tis hard work."

"Aye, that it is," said Mrs. Boyd, nodding vigorously. "But now that I am in London in the Queen's Theater, I find it very good work indeed. But not long before, I was with a troupe of traveling players, going about the provinces, playing here and there for a pittance and being insulted by country louts. Well, my lady, I cannot recommend it to anyone."

"I should think not," agreed Verity, "although there are times when I find myself imagining I should like the adventure of traveling about the kingdom, seeing new places. Did you not find it exciting, Mrs. Boyd?"

"Oh, my lady, I found it exhausting most of the time," replied Mrs. Boyd with a broad smile. At that moment servants arrived with tea. As she took up her cup, Mrs. Boyd found herself very glad that she had goaded Maria into calling upon Lady Verity. It was quite wonderful sitting there in the drawing room conversing with Lady Verity, who was obviously a very grand young lady despite her surprising lack of pretension. "But Mrs. Fleming tells me your ladyship is a playwright," said Mrs. Boyd. Verity regarded the woman in surprise. Noting how Maria frowned at her, the blond-haired actress realized she had made a gaffe. "Oh, I am sorry," she murmured in confusion.

"That is quite all right. Who told you that, Mrs. Boyd?"

Mrs. Boyd looked uneasy. "Mrs. Fleming said that Lord Ranley told her you had sent a play for him to read."

Verity looked at Maria. "Lord Ranley told you that?"

Maria nodded. "Oh, I shall not tell another soul, my lady."

"Nor shall I, my lady," said Mrs. Boyd hastily. "I know how disappointed you must have been—"

"Disappointed?"

"With Lord Ranley thinking your play so bad, my lady."

Verity almost choked on her tea. "He told you that my play was bad?"

"He did say so," said Mrs. Fleming. "I am sorry, Lady Verity."

Verity could not hide her indignation. So Ranley was telling people that she was a playwright! And a bad one at that! She had not taken him for a gabblemonger, but here he was revealing the secret she had taken such great care to hide.

"I beg your pardon, my lady." Weeks entered the room much to the relief of both of the actresses. "Lord Dorchester is here, my lady."

"Dorchester?" Verity looked at Mrs. Boyd and Maria. "I am sure you ladies would enjoy meeting my fiancé. By all means show his lordship in, Weeks."

When Dorchester entered the drawing room, he caught sight of Maria Fleming and her companion. The marquess was too well-bred to express the horror he felt at realizing that Verity was having tea with London's most notorious actress and another woman, who by the look of her was also a member of that disreputable profession. He only frowned slightly and proceeded toward his fiancée.

"Gerald," said Verity. "How lucky that you have come.

Ladies, I have the honor to present my fiancé, the Marquess of Dorchester. Gerald, this is Mrs. Fleming and Mrs. Boyd." Dorchester adopted an expression of aristocratic disdain. He nodded at the actresses, but did not say a word. "You are just in time to join us for tea."

Noting Dorchester's demeanor, Maria decided that they were fast outwearing their welcome. She put down her teacup. "How do you do, my lord? What a pity that Mrs. Boyd and I have to be going."

"You have to be going?" said Verity, her voice expressing great disappointment.

"Yes, Lady Verity. But I do want to thank you for your kindness."

"Indeed, yes, my lady," said Mrs. Boyd. "Thank you so much for tea."

The visitors rose and took their leave of Verity, hastening past Dorchester. When they were gone, the marquess frowned at his fiancée.

"Gerald, I pray you cease scowling at me like a bad-tempered schoolmaster. Sit down and have some tea."

Dorchester remained standing. "I could not believe my eyes, Verity. You were entertaining those women in this house! Good God, my girl! Have you gone mad? Where is Lady Benbrook?"

"She is resting. And don't fly up into the boughs, Gerald. What is all the fuss about?"

" 'Pon my honor," sputtered Dorchester. "Those women are actresses! They are not respectable company for you. What will everyone think when it becomes known the sort of persons you invite to tea?" He shook his head. "Yesterday I came here and found you with that rogue Ranley. And if that weren't bad enough, today I find you chatting with two painted, disreputable . . . actresses. I warn you, Verity, this fascination of yours for the theater is quite unacceptable. You have always been too little aware of your position in society. You have always been too familiar with inferiors.

"I will not have you behaving in this way when we are married. When you are Marchioness of Dorchester, you will behave with the proper dignity."

"I will behave as I please," said Verity, rising from her chair and eyeing him fiercely. "If you so disapprove of me, I suggest you find another bride, Gerald."

"I do not want another bride, Verity," said Dorchester. "I simply want you to behave in a manner befitting your station."

"Gerald, I do not wish to quarrel with you. I suggest you go."

The marquess paused and then nodded. "If that is what you want, Verity. I shall return when you have had time to reflect upon this. Good day to you." He turned and abruptly departed. Verity sank back down in her chair. However had she agreed to marry him, she asked herself. Frowning, she sat in gloomy silence.

14

After rising from her nap, Lady Benbrook went downstairs. She found Verity sitting in the drawing room looking pensive. "What is the matter, my dear?" asked the countess, coming to sit beside her daughter on the sofa.

"Nothing, Mama. It is only that I have had a quarrel with Gerald."

"He was here?"

"Yes, not long ago. He was very angry. Of course, I was angry, too."

"What happened?"

Verity looked over at her mother. "Gerald does not think Mrs. Fleming fit company for me."

"Mrs. Fleming the actress?" said Lady Benbrook. "My heavens, Verity, she is not fit company for you. Why would you even discuss such a thing?"

"Because, Mama, I have just had Mrs. Fleming and her friend Mrs. Boyd to tea."

"They were here?" said the countess. "You admitted such persons and offered them tea? Oh, Verity."

"Do not look so disapprovingly at me, Mama. Gerald was disapproving enough for one day. I see nothing wrong with being hospitable. And Mrs. Fleming and Mrs. Boyd were so terribly interesting. They are not monsters."

"Perhaps they are not monsters, but that does not make it acceptable to admit them to one's drawing room. I shall insist that you show better judgment in the future, my dear. You knew very well how your father and I would feel about you having such persons to tea. One cannot fault Dorchester for being upset."

"But I can fault him for acting in such a pompous, boorish fashion. Truly, Mama, he is quite insufferable. I know I shall be miserable being married to him. And I shall make him very unhappy as well. By my faith, I cannot imagine why he wishes to marry me."

"He is fond of you, my dear."

"Is he?" said Verity thoughtfully.

"Indeed he is. Now, my dear, these quarrels are quite trivial. Dorchester will forget about it very quickly."

"Perhaps he will," returned Verity, "but I shall not."

"I do hope you are not going to say you refuse to marry Gerald, Verity."

Verity sighed and adopted a tragic look. "No, Mama, I am resolved to my miserable fate. You and Papa may rest assured that I will go to my doom like a soldier."

"Oh, Verity."

She rose from the sofa. "I pray you excuse me, Mama. I should prefer to be alone."

As the countess watched her daughter retreat from the drawing room, she frowned and for the first time wondered if forcing Verity to marry Dorchester could be a grave mistake.

Verity did not see Dorchester for a few days but when he finally arrived at Benbrook House, he was eager to restore himself to his fiancée's good favor. He was glad to find that Verity was polite and appeared to have forgotten the incident with Mrs. Fleming. Lady Benbrook was very much relieved that the two of them were behaving in a civil fashion and that the unfortunate little spat was behind them.

She was also relieved that Verity said little about her impending wedding and expressed no objections to assisting with the many preparations for her departure. There were many things to see to, clothes to be readied, shopping to be done, and decisions to be made as to what things Verity would bring to her new home. There were also the usual social obligations to be attended as well as appointments with dressmakers and hairdressers. The days were, therefore, busy and passed quickly.

The day of the Princess de la Bretonne's ball soon arrived. Verity had been looking forward to the occasion for everyone in society was talking about it. The Prince Regent himself as well as a number of other royal personages would be in attendance, a fact that made it especially exciting for lesser mortals.

Verity's ball gown was a very grand example of the dressmaker's art. Fashioned from gleaming white satin, the low-cut bodice of the high-waisted creation was decorated with lace. Satin rosettes and lace adorned the skirt and short sleeves of the dress.

It was a very splendid gown indeed, thought Nell as she assisted her mistress into it. "You look beautiful, my lady," said the maid. "There will be no one at the ball to hold a candle to your ladyship."

Verity studied her appearance in the mirror as Nell fastened her glittering emerald necklace about her neck and then adjusted the wreath of satin roses that she wore on her head. "I assure you, Nell, I will be far outshone by all the grand beauties of society. There are a good many of them to be sure." She turned away from the mirror and took the white gloves and ivory-trimmed fan that Nell handed to her.

"I do hope your ladyship has a nice time at the ball."

"Oh, I do intend to do so, Nell. After all, this is my last ball as a free woman. When next I attend such an affair, I

shall be Lady Dorchester. I suppose that is a very grand thing
to be. His lordship certainly believes so."

"Oh, my lady," said Nell sympathetically.

"Well, I shall not think of such things tonight. I shall
gossip with everyone and I shall dance with all the young
gentleman and be extremely merry."

"That is good, my lady," said Nell uncertainly. Verity's
mood seemed to be shifting back and forth that day from
gaiety to gloominess and it was difficult to know how to react.
She was glad when Verity left her and she could busy herself
in tidying the dressing room before joining her fellow
servants below stairs.

The Benbrooks left very late for the ball due to Lady
Benbrook's last-minute unhappiness with her coiffure, which
was fortunately put right by Nell Dawson's hairdressing
skills. As the carriage made its way to the residence of the
Princess de la Bretonne, the earl complained that they were
in danger of arriving even later than the Prince Regent himself. The countess and Verity kept assuring Lord Benbrook
that they were in no danger of committing this unforgiveable breech of etiquette, and as they entered the magnificent
residence of the Princess de la Bretonne, it was obvious that
they were not the only late arrivals.

There were still many latecomers alighting from fine
carriages and Verity could not help but be caught up in the
excitement as they entered the grand house. The princess's
home could properly be called a palace. It was vast and filled
with light from the thousands of candles ablaze on enormous
crystal chandeliers.

There was such a great crush of people on the marble staircase that ascended to the grand ballroom, the Verity felt like
one tiny ant swarming into a giant ant hill. Once she and
her parents had been announced and had entered the
enormous room, Verity looked about, scanning the glittering
crowd. An orchestra played, filling the ballroom with lively
music as ladies and gentlemen danced a mazurka.

"There is Dorchester," said Lord Benbrook. "He is standing with the duchess."

"Rose is a very good color for her, don't you think, Verity?" said Lady Benbrook, catching sight of her old friend. "And does not Gerald look so handsome?"

"Yes," returned Verity, looking toward the Duchess of Haverford and her son. "Gerald always looks handsome, Mama." Dorchester glanced toward them, and spotting his fiancée and her parents, he took his mother by the arm and started in their direction.

"Duchess," said Lord Benbrook, bowing to her grace. "How well you look."

"Yes, rose is your color, Kate," said the countess, smiling brightly at the duchess and Dorchester.

"You are too kind," returned the duchess, who then bestowed compliments upon Lady Benbrook's and Verity's appearances. "Does Verity not look lovely, Gerald?"

"Indeed so," said Dorchester, eager to join the conversation. "There is not a lady here to match you."

"Oh, Gerald, I do not expect such flummery from you," said Verity.

"It is hardly flummery," returned the marquess, pleased that his fiancée appeared to be in good spirits. "Why, look about. I am undoubtedly in the company of the prettiest ladies here." He cast a disapproving eye about the ballroom. "Indeed, I have seen some quite frightful gowns."

"Yes," said the duchess. "Mrs. Abercromby is wearing the most peculiar shade of yellow I have ever seen. And do look at Lady Phillippa Brent. She is dancing there with Sir John Marbury. I fancy they may think such dresses fit for society in Paris, but here in London, I do not think it is the thing at all."

Verity looked curiously at the dancers and found the lady in question. She was wearing a filmy low-cut creation, but Verity found it hardly scandalous. "And I daresay, Verity," continued the duchess, "that your friend Carolyn Billing-

ham's gown is utterly unflattering. Poor girl. She is so plain
and she has grown far too stout.''

"Carolyn is here?'' said Verity eagerly. ''I did not know
she was in town. Oh, I do wish to see her.''

Dorchester frowned. He did not like Carolyn Billingham,
nor did he consider her family's pedigree sufficiently aristocratic for intimate association. However, knowing that Verity
was very fond of Carolyn, he wisely refrained from saying
anything. He found himself thinking, however, that once they
were married, he would discourage the friendship. After all,
he considered the Billinghams to be provincial nobodies with
uncouth habits.

"Oh, I see Carolyn,'' said Lady Benbrook. ''Isn't that her
brother Harry with her?''

"Yes, Lady Benbrook,'' replied Dorchester. ''That is
Harry Billingham. I never could abide the fellow.''

Verity smiled. She knew that Dorchester had despised
Harry Billingham since childhood. They had all grown up
not very far from each other in Lancashire and had been
unavoidably thrown together a good deal. As boys, they had
fought many times, Harry always winning due to his larger
size and indifference to the niceties of fair play. ''Gerald,
shouldn't we go and see Carolyn and Harry?''

"I have no desire to waste my time on Harry Billingham,''
replied Dorchester testily.

"Nor do I,'' said Lord Benbrook. ''I have always said
Harry Billingham is a scoundrel. His own father thinks so
as well.''

"Well, I shall not ask anyone else to waste their time upon
the Billinghams, but I must go and see Carolyn. Do excuse
me.''

Before Dorchester or her father could protest, Verity
hurried off toward her friend. Carolyn Billingham let out
a squeal of delight at seeing her approach. She opened her
arms and embraced Verity tightly.

Carolyn Billingham was rather stout and unprepossessing.
Her countenance was marred by her too prominent front teeth

and decidedly weak chin. Carolyn's unruly brown hair had always plagued her with its tight natural curl that tended to frizz. Yet Carolyn's bright, cheery personality and brilliant smile made her popular in her Lancashire community. "Oh, Verity! How good it is to see you!"

"Why did you not tell me you were coming, Caro?"

"I did not have time. Mama and Papa did not wish to come. It was only my relentless hounding of them and Harry's promise to behave that finally convinced them. We just arrived yesterday. And to think that our first foray into society would be this ball! It is my cousin Mary's doing that we received invitations. You remember that she is married to Lord Rayburne, who is the brother of Mrs. Woodcliffe, who is a dear friend of the Princess de la Bretonne."

Verity laughed. "I am very glad you are here, however you managed it, Caro." She looked over at Harry Billingham. He was a large, broad-shouldered man of about thirty, carelessly dressed in well-worn evening clothes. "Good evening, Harry."

"Hello, Verity. You looked damned pretty. Where are Lord and Lady Benbrook?"

"Over there with Dorchester and the duchess."

"I can see why they didn't come with you then," said Harry with a grin. "I should like to talk, but you girls would prefer I was not hanging about. I know how you females chatter. And there is a particular lady I have my eye on."

"I thought you had said you promised to behave, Harry," said Verity with mock severity.

Harry laughed and took his leave. The two young ladies then plunged eagerly into conversation. "Thank heaven you are here. I am having such a miserable time."

"But why, Caro?"

"We have been here for ages and I have not danced once. I should like to take a seat behind that potted palm over there, but Mama would scold me dreadfully. So I stand here terribly bored, trying to look gay and amused. And my feet are getting very sore. But now you are here and it will be fun."

"I do hope so, Caro," replied Verity. "But if it is not, we will hide behind the potted palm together."

Carolyn laughed. "Are you still to marry Dorchester on the twenty-seventh of the month, Verity?"

Verity nodded. "Oh, let us not speak of my wedding, Caro."

"Then you are still unhappy?"

"I am not happy about it, to be sure, but I am reconciled to it. But I beg you, say no more about it. You must tell me about yourself. How are your parents?"

"They are very well. They are here somewhere. I'm sure you will see them soon for Mama has been watching me like a hawk, hoping that some short-sighted gentleman will ask me to dance."

"Oh, Caro."

Carolyn laughed again. "Papa grumbled about coming to the ball. You know that he detests life in town. He cannot wait until he is back in Lancashire and it is hunting season. Mama said that . . ." Carolyn stopped in midsentence. "Verity, the most handsome man I have ever seen is coming toward us."

Verity turned her head and her blue eyes registered surprise. There making his way toward them was Ranley. "It is Lord Ranley," she said in what she hoped was an indifferent tone.

"Do you know him, Verity?"

"I have had the dubious honor of making his acquaintance," returned Verity.

If Ranley heard this remark as he neared the two young ladies, he gave no sign of it. He stopped before them and bowed to Verity. "Lady Verity."

"Lord Ranley." Verity tried to remain cool and collected as she regarded the baron. Carolyn Billingham had been right in her assessment of Ranley's appearance. He was, thought Verity, the most handsome man in England. He stood there in his perfectly tailored evening clothes, the very picture of the elegant fashionable gentleman. "Carolyn, may I present

Lord Ranley? My lord, this is my dear friend, Miss Billing-ham.''

"Your servant, Miss Billingham," said the baron, taking Carolyn's hand and bending over it.

Carolyn had never thought of herself as the sort of silly ninnyhammer who would have an attack of the vapors at the attentions of a good-looking man. She found herself ready to change her mind as Ranley flashed his famous smile at her. Verity looked over at her friend and then at the baron. How aggravating, she thought, that Ranley had the power to completely bedazzle even the most sensible of females. "It is a great honor to meet you, Lord Ranley," Carolyn managed to say. "Like Verity, I am a great admirer of yours." Verity thought her friend's inclusion of "like Verity" most unfortunate and she noted that the baron raised his dark eyebrows at her with an expression of faint amuse-ment. Carolyn continued. "I am so looking forward to seeing your play *Valiant Lady*."

"It is his lordship's greatest work," said Verity quickly. She smiled at Ranley, but was disappointed when he did not seem in the least irked by the remark.

"I do hope you will enjoy the play, Miss Billingham," said Ranley. "Lady Verity thinks very highly of it." He turned to Verity. "You are so kind to praise my poor efforts. I was hoping that you would honor me with a dance, Lady Verity."

Verity looked at him in some surprise. "Why, I could not possibly leave my friend."

"Nonsense, Verity," said Carolyn. "You could not disappoint Lord Ranley. I do not mind in the least."

Verity hesitated. She was not very happy with Ranley since learning that he had told Mrs. Fleming about her playwriting. She also knew that her father and Gerald would disapprove of her dancing with Ranley. After all, she was engaged to be married and Ranley did have a somewhat tarnished rep-utation where ladies were concerned. Deciding that she did not care one fig for what Dorchester would say, Verity replied, "Very well, Lord Ranley, I shall dance with you."

"You have my undying gratitude, Lady Verity," he said bowing dramatically. Verity tried hard not to smile and Ranley bowed to Carolyn. "It was a great pleasure meeting you, Miss Billingham. I do hope that you will save the next dance for me."

Carolyn smiled brightly. "I should be very happy to do so, Lord Ranley."

Then taking their leave, Ranley and Verity made their way toward the dance area. "I am most obliged to you for accepting me, Lady Verity." He looked over at her. "It appears that you have done so against your better judgment."

"I cannot know what you mean, sir."

"You do not look altogether pleased."

"You are too accustomed to females who appear ecstatically happy at your least attention."

Ranley smiled. "Perhaps so," he said.

Verity laughed in spite of herself. The mazurka ended and the orchestra began the next dance, a waltz. Ranley put his arm around her and took her hand. As she expected, the baron was an expert dancer. He waltzed flawlessly, leading her about the polished dance floor. "I am glad to see that you have suffered no ill effects from your fall from the horse."

"No, I am fully recovered," returned the baron. "And I shall work harder at my horseback riding."

"Indeed, sir, for it is evidently the only thing at which you do not excel." Ranley was not sure how to react to this remark. They continued dancing with the baron regarding Verity expectantly. "I am vexed with you, Lord Ranley," said Verity finally.

The baron looked into her blue eyes and raised his dark eyebrows. "I thought as much, but I should like to know why."

"I do not much appreciate your betraying my confidences."

"Have we shared confidences, Lady Verity?"

"Don't be odious. You told Mrs. Fleming that I write plays, and if that is not bad enough—for I expressly told you I wished this to be a secret—you also told her that I have no ability."

"Good God," said Ranley. "How did you know about that?"

"Mrs. Fleming told me over tea."

"You had Maria Fleming to tea?"

"You mean she did not tell you?"

"My dear Lady Verity, I have not seen Maria in some days. And in defense of my behavior, I must tell you that I told her about your play because I could think of no better explanation for you and me being together at the Crown and Anchor. You recall that she saw us there. I trust you prefer the play explanation to the conclusion that Maria was drawing."

Verity feared she was blushing. "You did not have to say the play was dreadful."

Ranley laughed. "That was Billy again, not I." When she regarded him skeptically, he laughed again. "Upon my word of honor."

"Oh," said Verity, smiling at him. "You must tell Mr. Hawkins that I am very displeased."

"I promise I shall do so." He smiled at her and Verity sounded a warning to herself. It was very dangerous finding oneself in Ranley's arms. Certainly, few women had ever had the strength to resist him, and as they whirled about the dance floor, Verity began to feel that she did not wish to resist him. She was disappointed but then relieved when the music ended and the baron escorted her back to where Carolyn was standing.

By this time, however, Carolyn was not standing alone. She had been joined by the Benbrooks, Dorchester, and the Haverfords. Ranley greeted the others with his usual aplomb, ignoring Dorchester's glowering looks. Since Carolyn had promised him the next dance, he did not linger, but escorted the delighted Miss Billingham away from the others.

"Why do I find myself always seeing or hearing about that fellow?" said Lord Benbrook, watching Ranley and Carolyn with disapproval.

"He is Brutus Ranley, after all," said Lady Benbrook. The duchess nodded in agreement and Verity smiled at Dorchester's frown. The rest of the evening went by very quickly. After dancing with Ranley, Carolyn Billingham was surprised to find that she no longer had to face the rest of the evening as a wallflower. Ranley's attention had peaked the interest of a number of other gentlemen who were accustomed to aping the baron's every move. She danced a good many other dances and met an amiable young man with whom she had a most amusing conversation. Indeed, had the young man not suffered so in comparison with Ranley, Carolyn might have found herself setting her cap for him.

Verity had never had the problem of lacking dance partners, but she realized that Ranley's interest turned the attention of most everyone in the room upon her. She was deluged with requests for dances and overwhelmed by dashing young men offering to obtain glasses of punch for her.

The Prince Regent arrived at the ball very late and everyone stopped to pay obeisance to their sovereign. Verity thought the prince looked very regal as he made his way across the ballroom accepting the bows and curtsies of the guests with a courtly nod. His Royal Highness was growing rather corpulent, but his whalebone stays and well-cut evening dress did a good job of making him look imposing rather than stout.

Verity noted along with everyone else that the prince stopped and spoke with Lord Ranley for a very long time. This mark of the royal favor was not surprising, for royal George had long been a great patron of the theater and a great admirer of Brutus Ranley. Once the prince had been properly greeted, the ball resumed once again.

Ranley approached Verity for another dance, but at that

time Dorchester was standing guard over his fiancée. The marquess informed the baron that Verity had promised him the next dance and Ranley bowed to Verity and departed.

By this time it was growing very late and Verity was becoming irritated with Dorchester. They danced a country dance that went so fast and changed partners so frequently that there was no opportunity for conversation. Considering her fiancé's surly expression, Verity was very glad she did not have to say much to him. Then she was surrounded by other ardent admirers and the marquess could only stand about scowling.

When Verity finally arrived home and went to bed, she lay for a long time thinking about the ball despite the late hour. She had never had such a time, she decided, smiling into the darkness of her room. And after dancing the dance with Ranley over in her head many times, Verity finally fell into an exhausted sleep.

15

The afternoon after the ball, Dorchester arrived at Benbrook House. Lord and Lady Benbrook welcomed him eagerly into the drawing room and sent a servant to fetch Verity from her room. "It was a lovely ball, was it not?" said the countess after the three of them had settled down into their chairs. "I so enjoyed myself. I daresay it was the finest event of the season."

Dorchester nodded politely, but made no comment on an event which he considered an unpleasant memory. He had not enjoyed himself. Indeed, he had been quite upset with Verity's dancing with every buck who asked her as if it were her first Season and she were not an engaged lady. Lady Benbrook continued to talk about the ball, pausing every once in a while to allow the gentlemen to interject a remark.

When Verity appeared in the doorway, Dorchester rose politely to his feet. "Good afternoon, Verity."

"Good afternoon, Gerald."

"We were just talking of the ball, my dear," said the countess. "Do sit down beside dear Dorchester." Verity obediently took a place on the sofa next to her fiancé. She noted that the marquess looked rather solemn. "I do expect, now that you are here, Verity, Dorchester would prefer to speak about your wedding."

"A very good idea," said Lord Benbrook. "It is scarcely more than a week away."

This remark made Verity frown, but she said nothing. "I do believe everything is arranged," said the countess. "What a glad day it will be to see my dear girl a bride. I am so glad that your new home will be so close to us in town."

Verity looked over at her future husband and a sense of doom came over her. Scarcely listening as the marquess talked about his new London house, Verity came to attention when Dorchester remarked, "But we will not be staying there. I thought we would go to Lancashire as soon as possible, the day after the wedding I should think. I must oversee the improvements to Ridgewood Manor and it is quite essential that we go there at once. It is quite habitable now, of course, but I am adding a wing as it is too small at present."

"You cannot mean you wish to leave town so soon," said Verity. "The Season is not ended."

"It cannot be helped," said Dorchester matter-of-factly. "But you still have a week to make ready."

Verity frowned at him, thinking she would be utterly miserable at Ridgewood Manor, away from her friends and family. Why on earth had he come up with such an idea except to vex her?

The countess, noting her daughter's expression, began to talk about what a pleasant residence Ridgewood Manor was. She had been there many times, she said, and even if it was rather remote and a trifle far from Benbrook Castle, that did not signify in the least since they would visit her often and she them. The earl chimed in that he had hunted there many years ago and it was the best sport one could ever hope to have.

Verity sat sullenly regarding her parents as if they were conspirators. Did they not realize that the idea of marriage to Dorchester was only tolerable because she assumed that things would go on much the same as before? She had thought that she would reside at the ducal residence of Haverford, the neighboring estate to her parents' country home. She had not expected that Dorchester would take on the role of lord and master, deciding where they would live without even a "by your leave."

"I should prefer to stay at Haverford," said Verity. "And I should prefer to stay in town for some weeks after the wedding."

Dorchester turned and regarded her as if she were a wayward child. "I fear that is not possible, Verity. All is arranged."

Verity checked the angry retort she was about to utter. She did not want to argue with Dorchester there in front of her parents. She sat silently, but as Dorchester smiled a condescending smile at her, Verity made a decision. She would not marry Gerald, she told herself. She did not care what her parents said. They might hate her if they would, but nothing would make her marry him.

The countess changed the subject at that point and the conversation turned to other matters. After a time, Dorchester took his leave and when he was gone, Lord and Lady Benbrook regarded their daughter with unmistakeable disapproval. "I do think you could have been less disagreeable, Verity," said the countess sternly.

"I disagreeable?" said Verity. "It is Gerald who is disagreeable." She paused and then continued. "I know that you will be very angry, but I have decided that I will not marry Gerald."

The earl's mouth dropped open in surprise. "What the devil!" he cried.

"Verity," said Lady Benbrook. "We have quarreled over this so many times that it is quite tiresome. You have said you would marry Gerald, and that is that."

"I will marry anyone else, but not him. Why on earth are you so determined that I marry Gerald?"

"Because," said the earl, "the matter has been decided years ago. You know very well that the duke and I agreed that you and Dorchester would wed when you were a tiny child. All the arrangements have been made. Everything is settled."

"I am very sorry that the duke will be disappointed, Papa, but there is nothing you can do to force me to marry Gerald. I am adamant. I will not marry him."

The earl's face grew red. "It is too late for this, my girl," he said. "I have indulged you far too long, allowing you to do as you please. You are behaving as a spoiled child. I will not tolerate it. And you will marry Dorchester as you said you would. By my honor, you will do so or you will be no daughter of mine. Now go to your room and do not come out until you have come to your senses."

Surprised by the vehemence of her father's words, Verity looked to her mother for assistance. When the countess remained mute, Verity rose from the sofa and hurried from the room.

Once inside her bedchamber, she paced about the room, a look of grim resolution on her face. She would not marry him, she told herself, even if it meant her father would disown her, and considering his expression, it was likely that he would do just that.

Verity folded her arms in front of her. She did not care if she was disowned and disgraced. If need be, she would make her own way in the world. After all, did she not have one hundred pounds? That was a good deal of money, enough to live for a long time if one lived modestly somewhere. She could write other plays and make a living of her own. There would be no need to have a husband bossing one about.

Verity nodded to herself as she considered the matter. Then she went to the dresser table and unlocked the hidden drawer. There, safe and sound, was the purse with the money

Hawkins had given her. Taking the coins from their hiding place, Verity smiled and then rang for Nell.

When the maid appeared, she found her mistress in the dressing room rummaging through her wardrobe. "Good heavens, Nell, none of these things will do at all. Everything is too . . . fashionable."

"Indeed, my lady," said Nell, suppressing a smile. "You wish to wear something unfashionable?"

"I wish to look ordinary, Nell. Yes, ordinary and non-descript. I do not wish to attract any attention."

This remark alarmed Nell. "Whatever can your ladyship be thinking of doing?"

"Why, I am running away, Nell."

"My lady!" cried the maid. "You cannot mean it."

"Oh, I do indeed," returned Verity, continuing to look through her clothes. "Why is there nothing plain and severe? Why on earth have I selected such a collection of bows and lace and silly fripperies?"

Nell regarded her mistress with a worried look. "My lady, I beg you to sit down. You are overwrought."

"I am nothing of the sort," said Verity. "I am quite calm and I have thought everything over very carefully. I have decided that I will not wed Lord Dorchester. That is my final decision."

"Indeed, my lady," said Nell uncertainly.

"My father and mother have said I must marry him or I will be disowned. I have no desire to live in a household where I am treated in such an infamous manner by a father who behaves like a medieval tyrant."

"Surely his lordship will not force you to marry against your will, my lady," said Nell. "He must have lost his temper."

"You don't understand, Nell," said Verity firmly. "I have put off this marriage for two years. My father has lost patience and I daresay I do not blame him. But I will not marry anyone who is not of my own choosing. And since my parents can no longer bear to see me unmarried, I have no choice but to run away. I cannot ask you to accompany me, Nell. It would not be fair.''

"Your ladyship could not go alone," said Nell stoutly. "I think it most unwise for you to leave here, but if you can not be persuaded to give up this plan, I shall go with you."

"Dear Nell," said Verity, giving her maid a quick hug. "I know you think me perfectly crack-brained, but I assure you, it is essential I go. And I do have the money from the play. We shall be able to live on that. And I shall write other plays and we will do splendidly."

"But where will we go?"

"I am not quite certain of that yet, Nell," said Verity, "but I have some ideas. Now we have so much to do that we must make haste. I wish to be gone by the morning."

"By the morning!"

"Yes, the sooner we are away the better. But I do wish I had something I could wear. Oh, I just had an idea. What about the attic?"

"Oh, my lady, there is nothing in the attic but some old clothes her ladyship did not wish to discard."

Verity brightened. "Do go and fetch them, Nell. But take care that no one sees you. And not a word to anyone."

"Of course not, my lady," said the maid. As she took her leave of her mistress, and stealthily made her way to the attic, Nell Dawson wondered if both she and her mistress had lost their senses.

16

Whatever misgivings Nell had had about her mistress's plan to run away were magnified by the bad weather that greeted them when they left Benbrook House at dawn. As Verity and Nell hurried down the street, blustery winds blew at their cloaks and threatened to carry away their bonnets. A light rain was falling, but the sky was so dark that Nell worried that a downpour would soak them at any moment.

Both of the young women carried bulky traveling bags that grew heavier with each step. After they had walked for what seemed to Nell a very long way, Verity spoke. "There it is, Nell. There is the chaise I hired."

"Thank Providence," muttered Nell. "I do not think I could have gone much farther, my lady."

"Nor could I," said Verity, stopping and putting down one of her valises to wave at the man sitting in the chaise. "I do wish I could have had the chaise come to the house, but I daresay someone might have seen it. And, indeed, I did not wish the driver to know he was taking passengers from Benbrook House. We must take care that no one suspects who we are.''

''Yes, my lady,'' returned Nell.

''And Nell,'' said Verity, taking up her case once again as the chaise driver came toward them. ''Do not call me 'my lady.' ''

Before Nell could question her mistress as to what she was now to be called, the driver stood before them. ''Be you Mrs. Trelawney?'' he said.

''Yes.''

The man took the bags from Verity. ''Come along then, ma'am.'' He helped both the young ladies into the chaise.

Once seated in the vehicle, Nell felt somewhat better. ''Mrs. Trelawney?'' she whispered.

Verity nodded and replied in a low voice. ''It is a good name, don't you think? Oh, I quite agonized over what to call myself, Nell. It is not easy choosing a name for oneself. I think Mrs. Trelawney has a nice romantic ring to it. But what shall we call you?''

''Could I not be Nell anymore, my—that is, ma'am?''

''Why yes, Nell, but we must have a new surname for you. Have you any ideas?''

Nell appeared thoughtful. ''I did not know I would have a new name, ma'am. I shall think on it.''

Verity smiled as her servant pondered the matter. The carriage continued through the streets, arriving finally at the White Bear Inn. This establishment was a coaching inn of some reputation, which was the terminus for coaches arriving from and departing for destinations throughout the kingdom. By this time rain was falling heavily. Despite the early hour, there were a number of people milling about obtaining tickets and waiting to begin journeys. The chaise driver helped the ladies down and led them to shelter. ''Shall I fetch your tickets, ma'am?''

Nodding, Verity took some coins from her reticule. ''That would be good of you.''

"It was the coach for Truro you were wanting, was it not, ma'am? It will be here shortly."

Verity, who was not at all sure which coach she should take, looked thoughtful. She was vaguely aware that Truro was a town in Cornwall. "Why, yes, that is the coach I want. How clever of you to know."

"Why, ma'am, I was only guessing, but with a name like Trelawney . . . 'Tis a good Cornish name. And I know the coach for Truro be leaving shortly."

"I should be most grateful to you if you would obtain our tickets, sir," said Verity not wishing to discuss Cornish names with the driver. He nodded and was off.

"Cornwall, my lady?" said Nell. "Is that not a very long way away?"

"No farther than Lancashire, Nell. Indeed, I don't think it is as far. In any case, it is the perfect place. No one would ever suspect we would go there. Why, I do not know a soul there. Yes, it is the very spot for us. And the coach is leaving soon. Indeed, everything is going remarkably well."

Nell looked over at her mistress and wondered if it was too late for her to back out of this wild adventure. Surely it was lunacy to go off to some wild place like Cornwall with no idea whatsoever where they would live or what they would do. Verity smiled confidently, dispelling some of Nell's doubts with her look of assurance.

After a short time the chaise driver was handing their luggage to one of the coachmen who deposited it on top of the enormous stagecoach. He then assisted Nell and Verity into the cumbersome vehicle and wished them good journey. As she eyed her fellow passengers Verity was filled with excitement. This was a real adventure, the first she had ever had.

Verity smiled benevolently at her fellow passengers. Seated across from her was a sour-looking young man dressed like a dandy. Beside him was an attractive woman in a plum-colored pelisse who was evidently accompanied by an older man who Verity supposed was her father. Seated next to Nell was a stout red-faced man who greeted them all in a jovial manner, proclaiming that they had a long journey ahead of them and he hoped that they would find each other good company. When his remark solicited little response, he fell silent.

The coach started with a lurch and soon they were on their way through the streets of town. Verity was glad she was seated beside the window. She absently regarded the shops they were passing. Due to the early hour, most were still shuttered and dark.

Verity hoped that she looked sufficiently ordinary. She was dressed in a plain black dress which was barely visible beneath her heavy cloak of gray wool. Upon her head was a simple gray bonnet whose only adornment was a bit of gray satin ribbon.

The occupants of the coach rode in silence for some time, but when the vehicle had reached the outskirts of the metropolis, the man sitting beside Nell could no longer bear the quiet. "Shall we not introduce ourselves?" he said. "I do think it a good idea since we will be two days in each other's company. Such enforced intimacy as this allows a breach of etiquette." The sour-looking young man scowled at him, apparently displeased at the prospect of abandoning his anonymity. Undaunted, the stout man continued. "My name is Martin Prescott."

The lady in the plum-colored pelisse answered in a most civil fashion. "How do you do, sir? I am Mrs. Baldwin. This is my husband, Mr. Baldwin. And this young man is my stepson, Richard."

"An honor to meet you," exclaimed Mr. Prescott.

They turned and looked expectantly at Verity and Nell. "I am Mrs. Trelawney, and this is . . . Miss Reynolds." Verity hoped Nell would not mind the name she had chosen. Certainly they could change it later.

The convivial Mr. Prescott was very happy now that the introductions were made. "I daresay even such a long journey as this will seem very short in the company of three such lovely ladies. By my honor, I can scarcely believe my good fortune to be accompanying three such beauties as you ladies.''

Verity and the other women acknowledged this compliment graciously, but young Mr. Richard Baldwin eyed Prescott as if he thought him the greatest fool imaginable.

"Are you related to the Trelawneys of Newquay, Mrs. Trelawney?'' said Mrs. Baldwin, smiling at Verity. "I am acquainted with Sir Thomas Trelawney.''

"I do believe my late husband was distantly related to them," said Verity. "I fear I do not know any of his relations in Cornwall. To be sure he had a great many of them, but as I have never been there before, I have not had occasion to make their acquaintance.''

"My condolences on your bereavement, Mrs. Trelawney,'' said Prescott.

"You are very kind, sir,'' said Verity, adopting what she hoped was a suitably tragic expression.

Nell listened to her mistress with increasing admiration. How easily Verity talked of her fictitious dead husband. Of course, Verity was a playwright and such things came naturally to her.

"Are you traveling to Cornwall to visit your late husband's family, Mrs. Trelawney?'' said Mrs. Baldwin.

"Oh, I do not wish to impose upon them. And you see, my husband's family did not approve of our marriage.'' Verity noted with satisfaction the interest this remark generated among her listeners. She sighed.

"It is clear they had never met you, Mrs. Trelawney,'' said Prescott gallantly, "for surely had they done so, they would have heartily approved of having such a fine lady as yourself in their family.''

"You are too kind, Mr. Prescott,'' said Verity.

"Families can be so difficult,'' said Mrs. Baldwin, casting a significant look at her stepson. "It is very hard to please everyone.''

Verity nodded. "That is so very true, Mrs. Baldwin."
Although she was enjoying her role as tragic young widow,
Verity thought it prudent to divert the conversation from
herself. She asked Mrs. Baldwin if she resided in Cornwall.
The query was answered in the affirmative, allowing Mrs.
Baldwin opportunity to discourse at great length on life in
the west country.

Her words encouraged Mr. Prescott to speak about his
business in Cornwall. Since he was a loquacious gentleman,
one thing led to another and soon the passengers knew as
much about Mr. Prescott as they knew about their most
intimate friends. It was clear that young Richard Baldwin
had no desire to know anything at all about that gentleman;
he frowned for some time and then fell asleep.

The stagecoach stopped for a change of horses and the
passengers had an opportunity to stretch their legs and have
a bit of refreshment at an inn. They were well clear of the
city and the countryside stretched out before them, green and
fine. Verity found herself relaxing. It had been the right thing
to do, she reflected. She had freed herself from her marriage
to Dorchester. She tried not to think of her parents and was
glad when Mr. Prescott came forward and assisted her and
Nell back into the coach.

The Earl of Benbrook was roused from his bedchamber
at ten o'clock, an exceedingly early hour from his lordship's
point of view. He snarled at his butler, demanding to know
what earthly reason would cause him to be interrupted from
his rest. The servant's reply caused the earl to sit bolt upright
in bed. "What do you mean, Lady Verity is gone!"
exclaimed Benbrook.

"She is not here, m'lord, nor is Nell Dawson. We have
searched everywhere, m'lord. No one has seen them. We
wondered what was afoot when Nell didn't stop by as usual
in the servants' hall this morning. One of the maids found
this note addressed to your lordship."

"Good God," said the earl, taking the note from the man's

hand. Tearing it open, Benbrook read the missive. "Does Lady Benbrook know about this, Weeks?"

The butler shook his head. "I thought it best to inform your lordship first."

"Good," said the earl. He looked down at the note and read it again. It said, "Dear Mama and Papa, I know you will be frightfully angry. I cannot blame you, but you must know that I cannot bear the idea of marrying Gerald. I do not love him, and I know that I should be miserable if I submitted to the marriage. I would have made Gerald miserable as well.

"That is why I have gone off. I cannot tell you where I have gone, for, indeed, I am not certain where I am going. Nell is with me, but you must not blame her, for she tried to dissuade me from such a drastic course of action.

"Do not worry about me for I shall be fine. I have sufficient means to take care of myself if I live simply. I shall write you and in time I shall let you know where I am. I pray you will not hate me. Your disobedient but loving daughter, Verity."

Rising from his bed, the earl shouted at the butler to fetch his valet. After hurriedly dressing, he assembled a number of the male servants to begin a search. The commotion awakened the countess, who came downstairs in her dressing gown to see what was the matter. Lady Benbrook was quite distraught at the news. Clutching Verity's note to her bosom, she collapsed on the drawing room sofa, causing her maid Antoinette to run wildly from the room to obtain smelling salts. Once her ladyship's senses were restored, she burst into tears, wailing that Verity would surely come to harm and that her husband had been a monster to drive her from her home.

His wife's behavior did little to improve his lordship's temper. Gruffly ordering the countess to calm herself, the earl sent the servants out to make discreet inquiries about town. Not able to sit still himself, the earl called for his carriage and set out to join the search.

Once her husband had gone, Lady Benbrook paced about the house in agitation. Despite Antoinette's assurances that her young ladyship could not have gone far, the countess was very upset. She knew her daughter and was well aware that she was capable of succeeding in most things. If Verity was resolved to run away, Lady Benbrook did not doubt that she was half across the kingdom by now.

Time passed very slowly that morning. Too upset to have any breakfast, the countess continued to pace about and worry about her headstrong offspring. When she was sufficiently calm to think, her ladyship considered the matter, wondering if Verity might have confided in anyone. Thinking of Verity's friend, Carolyn Billingham, Lady Benbrook decided to pay a call upon that young lady. Accompanied by Antoinette, her ladyship appeared at the door of the Billinghams' residence.

Although Carolyn was very surprised to hear that Lady Benbrook had come at such an early hour, she did not hesitate to see her. Joining her in the Billinghams' drawing room, Carolyn saw immediately that the older woman was very much upset. "Whatever is the matter, Lady Benbrook?"

"Dear Carolyn, something quite dreadful has happened. Verity has flown off."

"Good heavens, Lady Benbrook!"

"Yes, she has left us a note, but no one has the least idea where she has gone. I am very worried."

"Indeed so, Lady Benbrook. But why has she run off and where could she possibly go?"

The countess frowned. "Oh, Carolyn, I am sure you know she did not wish to marry Dorchester. That is why she has run away. I was hoping you might have some idea where she has gone. You are her dearest friend. I hoped that Verity might have sent you a note."

Carolyn shook her head. "No, I have heard nothing from her. I pray you do sit down, ma'am. Will you have some tea?"

"That is good of you, Carolyn. I should like that."

Carolyn rang for a servant and after giving orders for tea, she sat down beside the countess. "Perhaps Verity will come back. Perhaps it is just a lark."

"I should box her ears if it were," said her ladyship severely. "No, I believe she is in deadly earnest. She left a note saying she was going off and that she had sufficient means to support herself. I cannot know what means she would have. Perhaps she took some of her jewelry. Oh, dear, you cannot think she means to sell her jewelry?"

"I do not know, Lady Benbrook," replied Carolyn thoughtfully. She hesitated. "You do not think that Verity has gone off with someone?"

"With someone? She has taken Nell with her."

"No, I mean with someone else."

"What on earth do you mean?"

Carolyn reddened. "I mean, perhaps she has gone off with a gentleman. Eloped."

Lady Benbrook's eyes grew wide in astonishment. "Eloped! Carolyn Billingham! With whom might she elope? Don't be absurd!"

"It was silly of me to mention it. It was only that after the ball, my brother told me of a rumor that he heard about Verity. I thought it nonsense. I should not mention it."

"You will mention it," demanded Lady Benbrook. "What rumor?"

Carolyn frowned. "It is quite ridiculous. There is a rumor that Verity was seen with a certain gentleman. I would think it complete bosh, but I did meet the gentleman at the ball and I saw how he looked at Verity, and I would not doubt that she is in love with him."

"Quit this silly prattle, girl, and tell me what you are talking about. Who is this gentleman?"

Carolyn hesitated. "Lord Ranley."

"Ranley?" Lady Benbrook was thunderstruck.

"Oh, it is most certainly nonsense."

The countess rose from her chair. "I'm sure it is nonsense, indeed. I must be off, Carolyn. And I beg you, do not say a word of this to anyone."

"I shall say nothing, Lady Benbrook. Do send me word the moment you find Verity."

The countess nodded and then took her leave. As she left the Billingham residence, Lady Benbrook's brow furled in concentration. She and her maid got into her phaeton and hurried away.

Ranley sat at his desk in the library carefully reading a page he held in his hand. After a short while, he placed it down on the desk atop a pile of similar papers. Folding his arms across his chest, the baron appeared pleased. He had finished his new play and, he told himself, it was damned good. It was a comedy, a broad farce actually, featuring a strong-willed heroine, a thick-headed hero, and a host of ridiculous secondary characters.

The female lead reminded the baron of Verity de Lacy. Not that she was entirely like Lady Verity, he reassured himself. No, but there were similarities. Or perhaps, wondered his lordship, was it that everyone and everything had of late been reminding him of Lady Verity?

He rose from his chair and walked over to the window. Yes, he admitted, he was spending an inordinate amount of time thinking about Verity. Indeed, considering how often his thoughts alighted on that young woman, one might have thought he was in love with the minx. Ranley dismissed this idea as absurd. It was not as though he was mooning about, unable to do anything, he reasoned. No, he had been remarkably productive, dashing off his play in record time. Yet, it was undeniable that Verity was seldom out of his thoughts no matter what he was doing.

The baron's musings were diverted by a stylish carriage that pulled up to the curb in front of his house. Ranley was surprised to recognize Lord Benbrook. Thinking it very odd that the earl would call upon him, Ranley was filled with curiosity.

Since he had left strict instructions that he would not receive anyone, the baron left the library and went directly to the entrance hall. There he intercepted the butler, who was just about to open the door. "I shall see this gentleman, Huntley. I'll be in the drawing room."

"Very good, my lord," said the servant, who waited for his master to vanish into the drawing room before opening the door.

"Is Lord Ranley in?" said Benbrook gruffly. "I am Lord Benbrook."

"His lordship will be happy to receive you, my lord."

Benbrook eyed the servant in some surprise. "Then he is here?"

"Yes, my lord. Do follow me."

Ranley thought his visitor looked very ill at ease as he entered the stylishly appointed drawing room. "Lord Benbrook," said the baron. "You do me great honor."

"Do I?" said the earl rather sourly. He looked around the drawing room. "It appears that I have come here for nothing. I told my wife it was absurd."

This remark caused Ranley to raise his dark eyebrows. "I should be grateful if you enlightened me, sir. What was absurd?"

Benbrook looked embarrassed. "I do not like airing my family problems before strangers. I see I have erred in coming here. Your pardon, sir. I will take no more of your time."

"Lord Benbrook," said the baron, "I pray you explain yourself. You cannot mean to rush off without telling me what has brought you here."

The earl frowned. "Oh, very well, but I must have your word as a gentleman that you will keep this matter a secret."

"I shall indeed," returned Ranley. His visitor's demeanor was beginning to worry him. Was something wrong with

Verity? "Do sit down, sir, and tell me what is the matter," said the baron, masking his concern with cool civility. "Would you have some sherry?"

"That would be much appreciated." Ranley nodded and poured a glass for his guest, who drank it in one gulp.

"I shall not sit, Ranley," said the earl, putting down his glass. "I shall not stay. I know you are acquainted with my daughter."

"Indeed I am, sir."

"She has run off."

"Run off, sir?"

"Yes, this morning. She left a note saying that she will not marry Dorchester. My God, can you imagine that? It was the finest match in England. There is not a girl in the kingdom who would not trade places with my Verity."

"But where did she go?" said Ranley. "Surely you must have some idea."

Benbrook shook his head. "Perhaps she has gone to Lancashire. I have sent a man to see. If she is not there, I have no clues whatsoever."

"If there is anything I can do, Lord Benbrook," said Ranley. "I shall be happy to assist you in looking for her. If you have come for my help, I assure you, sir, that you will have it."

Benbrook smiled. "That is not why I have come, Ranley. No, it was for an absurd reason. You see, my wife was told a rumor that is evidently moving about town. It is that you and my daughter are . . . and there was a suggestion that you had eloped with her."

"Good God!" exclaimed Ranley. "As you can see, I have not. And I assure you that Lady Verity would think that the most ridiculous idea! Why, we are scarcely acquainted. And in our brief acquaintance, the lady has made it very clear that she is totally disinterested in me."

"Forgive me for bothering you with such an absurdity. A father may be forgiven for making a fool of himself over his daughter. Do excuse me, Ranley."

After Benbrook had left, Ranley sat in the drawing room pondering the situation. Verity had run away! That was just like her, thought the baron. She was the most obstinate female he had ever met. And to think that Benbrook had had the idea that he had eloped with her! It was preposterous!

He considered the idea, imagining spiriting Verity de Lacy off to Gretna Green. The idea of being alone with her in a carriage was not unappealing. His mind pictured them arriving at some out-of-the-way inn where he would take her inside and cover her tantalizing lips with kisses. He conjured up Verity's blue eyes, and could see her raven hair spread out on her pillow, her clothes in disarray and her voluptuous charms awaiting his pleasure.

With some difficulty, the baron reined in his vivid imagination. What sort of man was he to be thinking thus when Verity was somewhere roaming about, very probably in serious trouble. Ranley looked thoughtful and then reassured himself that the Verity de Lacy he knew was in all likelihood taking very good care of herself.

17

On the second day of Verity's journey, the weather continued stormy. Rain fell steadily as the coach made its way along the narrow roads and the spirits of the travelers inside the vehicle flagged somewhat. Verity, still filled with a sense of adventure by the boldness of her flight, did not mind the weather. Happily enduring the bumps and jolts of the ride, she chatted amiably with Mrs. Baldwin and Mr. Prescott.

Nell was far less enthusiastic than her mistress about finding herself on a coach in western England. A sensible young woman, Nell worried about what they would do once they arrived in Cornwall. Verity did not seem at all concerned about such banalities as where they were to stay or how they would live. Nell wished she could be as confident as her mistress that all would be well.

It was early evening when the stagecoach pulled into the Cornish city of Truro. Verity looked out the window, eager to get a glimpse of their destination. Rain was by now falling heavily on the cobblestoned streets of the ancient town, causing most of its inhabitants to stay indoors.

Verity studied the neat houses and shops with interest. Truro was a charming place, picturesque and prosperous looking. Verity was filled with a sense of well-being as if benign Providence had brought them there.

When the coach pulled to a stop at the Black Swan Inn, the passengers alighted. Mrs. Baldwin had assured Verity that the Black Swan was a respectable establishment and that she and Nell should have no qualms about staying there. The affable Mrs. Baldwin had also invited them to stay with her for a time, but Verity had not wished to impose on her new friend. She did, however, promise Mrs. Baldwin that she would call upon her if she needed any assistance.

Verity also gratefully allowed Mr. and Mrs. Baldwin to escort her and Nell into the Black Swan and see that they had adequate lodgings. While his father and stepmother assisted Verity and Nell, Richard Baldwin stood outside looking irritated.

Verity took her leave of the Baldwins, thanking them profusely and assuring them that she would call at first opportunity. Although she was rather sorry to see the Baldwins go, she was glad to be rid of the disagreeable Richard.

Once inside their rooms at the inn, Verity took off her bonnet and tossed it on the bed. "We are here, Nell. Here in Cornwall! Whoever would expect it?"

"Indeed, no one, my lady," returned Nell.

"I pray you, Nell, do not call me 'my lady.' "

"I am sorry, ma'am."

"I do think Cornwall very beautiful. I know we will like it here."

"But where will we live?"

Verity shrugged. "Oh, Nell, you mustn't worry. We will stay here until we find a nice little cottage. I daresay it will not be too difficult. We have enough money for a long time.

And I shall write another play and send it to Mr. Hawkins. We will do very well."

Nell, who felt she knew more of the world than her mistress, could not be confident. However, she only nodded. "It is a very pretty town, Mrs. Trelawney."

"Indeed, it is, Miss Reynolds," returned Verity with a smile. "Now why don't you rest, Nell? It was a tiring journey. Listening to Mr. Prescott for all those miles was completely exhausting. Then we will have something to eat. I am quite famished."

"Will you not be needing anything, ma'am?"

"No, indeed, Nell. I think I shall write to my parents," said Verity. "I shall have to find a way to have the letter posted elsewhere, for I do not want the postmark to give us away. But I do not think that will be so difficult with so many travelers passing through here to London. No, I shall contrive something, Nell. But do rest for a while. I know how tired you are."

Nell nodded and left her mistress, retiring to the adjoining room where she lay down on the bed and soon fell asleep. Two hours later Verity and Nell made their way down to the public room of the inn for dinner.

The inn was quite uncrowded, with only a handful of persons partaking of the Black Swan's plain but ample fare. The innkeeper, having been asked by the Baldwins to look after Verity and Nell, was most solicitous, hurrying to escort them to his best table near the fire.

After being presented with a steaming beef pie, roast potatoes, and ale, Nell found her spirits improving. Since both the young ladies were famished after their journey, they ate heartily. "You see, Nell, this is not so bad," said Verity, taking a forkful of beef pie. "This inn is quite satisfactory until we find more permanent lodgings."

Nell, who was now fortified by the food and drink, appeared much more cheerful. "It is a very good inn, Mrs. Trelawney. Why, when I think of some of the inns we have stayed in coming back from Benbrook Castle . . ."

This remark caused Verity to launch into reminiscences about several rather rude accommodations they had endured and both the young ladies laughed merrily about bedbugs and surly inn servants. They were engaged in this discussion when they were startled by a shout. "You blackguard! I'll run you through with my steel!"

Verity and Nell looked over to see two men dressed in strange colorful garb rush into the center of the room. Both young ladies gasped to see that the men were brandishing sabers. "Stand and fight, coward!" cried one of the men, a burly youth with red hair and a florid countenance.

"Stand I shall and soon you will foul the earth no more with your presence, my lord!" shouted the other man, a tall blond giant with nordic features who spoke with a thick Germanic accent.

The two adversaries then fell upon each other with furious abandon, their swords coming together with great clangs. Verity could scarcely believe her eyes and Nell screamed as the two men continued to fight, rushing back and forth until the blond giant jumped up on one of the tables. Then he paused to glower at his opponent. Raising his sword dramatically, he cried, "Death to tyrants and long live Prince Odo!" Then, leaping from the table, he thrust his weapon into the burly youth.

"I am slain!" cried the victim. "Oh, I am slain!" Nell screamed again as the youth fell to the floor, writhed about for some time, and then lay still.

The perpetrator of the ghastly deed waved his oddly bloodless sword about triumphantly. "Thus die traitors and all who would abandon their lawful prince. And now the evil is done, the battle won!"

The other diners, who had watched the singular goings-on with keen excitement, now burst into applause. "Nell, you goose," said Verity. "It was a play." Nell breathed a sigh of relief as the recently slain youth jumped to his feet and bowed.

"Excellent, excellent," exclaimed a middle-aged gentleman, rising from his chair and going toward the two young men. He clapped each of them on the back. "And do not forget, ladies and gentlemen," he said loudly, "that our company will perform this wonderful play later during our stay in your fair city."

The few persons present nodded, their excited murmurings seeming to imply that they would not miss such a splendid show. The gentleman took the arms of the actors and led them toward a table. Passing Verity and Nell, he stopped. "I do beg your pardon, ladies. I must apologize, for it is evident that we have caused you distress."

Verity smiled. "One might have wished some notice of the entertainment, sir."

"Indeed so," said Nell. "I was nearly frightened to death."

The blond actor looked contrite. "Dear lady, I am so sorry if I alarmed you. I beg you to forgive me." This remark was given with such admirable sincerity and was spoken with such a charming accent that Nell could not help but reassure him that it was a matter of no consequence at all.

"And you were both excellent," said Verity. "I thought it quite wonderful."

"You are too kind," said the middle-aged man. "Perhaps you ladies would permit me to introduce myself. I am Josiah Mumford, at your service." He gestured toward the burly youth. "This is my son, Harold." Harold grinned and bowed to the ladies. "And this is Mr. Von Hoffman."

Von Hoffman came to attention and then bowed very low. "Your servant, ladies."

"I am Mrs. Trelawney," said Verity, smiling brightly at the gentlemen. "And this is Miss Reynolds."

"It is an honor to meet such charming ladies as yourselves," said Mumford.

"Perhaps you gentlemen will sit down with us," said Verity. Nell looked over at her mistress in some surprise, alarmed at her boldness, but Verity acted as if it was perfectly natural to invite strange gentlemen to join them at their table.

"You are too kind, Mrs. Trelawney." The three men took their seats, Von Hoffman sitting next to Nell and eyeing her with interest.

Verity turned her attention to Mr. Mumford. He was a stout man about forty years of age with red hair graying about the temples and a broad amiable smile. A loquacious gentleman, he needed little encouragement to speak about himself. He was, he informed the young ladies, the proud owner of an itinerant theater company, which was the equal of any that ever trod the stage at Covent Garden, Drury Lane, or the Queen's Theater.

Young Harold Mumford was a prodigious talent, according to his father. As an infant he was a marvel and now as a young man of scarcely sixteen, there was no end to his abilities.

After finally exhausting his praises of his son, Mumford nodded toward Von Hoffman, proclaiming him to be an actor nearly as gifted as the remarkable Harold. "How fortunate indeed," said Mumford, "that unhappy experiences in the Prussian army encouraged my dear friend Von Hoffman to abandon military life and make his way to England. What a tremendous gain for the English theater to have such a fine fellow upon the stage. I daresay my young friend is beginning a glorious career."

Von Hoffman nodded gravely at Mumford's words, but said nothing, apparently content to allow his employer to rattle on. "I do wish you great success while in Cornwall, Mr. Mumford," interjected Verity when Mumford paused enough to allow someone else to make a remark.

"That is kind of you, Mrs. Trelawney. I am happily optimistic despite certain unfortunate complications which may hinder our company from carrying on in the inimitable style to which we are accustomed to delighting our audiences."

"Unfortunate complications?" said Verity.

"Indeed yes, Mrs. Trelawney. You see, two of our cast

members departed hastily and surreptitiously but two nights ago. Unfortunately, they were our leading lady and one of our most notable actors. It has left an appalling gap in our company.''

"Run away together, they did," said Harold Mumford entering the conversation for the first time. "And he a married man!" he added with relish.

"Harold," said the elder Mumford reprovingly. "One should not tell tales."

"But that is what happened, Father," returned Harold. He nodded solemnly at Verity. " 'Twas a shocking business, as you might imagine."

"Indeed so," said Verity, nearly bursting into laughter at the young man's expression.

"But as I have told my father," continued Harold, "I can take on all of Mr. Willison's parts. But I cannot think who will take Miss Carrington's roles."

"We will discuss that later, my boy," said Mumford disapprovingly. "And I must ask you not to mention that lady's name. Yes, we will have to make do. I have no doubt that Miss Pettigrew can easily take on the roles left vacant by that lady who, for decency's sake, I shall not name."

Verity noted that this comment caused Von Hoffman to roll his eyes, his expression implying that he considered Miss Pettigrew to be a less than satisfactory replacement for the absent leading lady. "When one is in the theater, my dear ladies," continued Mumford, "one becomes accustomed to these sorts of crises. I do remember some years ago when a similar situation occurred when I was touring in the north. Our leading actor was, shall we say, incapacitated by overindulgence and could not go on. And do you know who replaced him?" Verity and Nell shook their heads and Mumford smiled and looked as though he was prepared to astonish them. "The famous Brutus Ranley, now Lord Ranley. I daresay you are familiar with the name."

"Indeed so," said Nell, her Miss Reynolds persona combined with the ale she had drunk making her uncharacteristically bold. "Mrs. Trelawney and I are acquainted with his lordship."

Verity gave a warning kick to Nell's shin, but it was too late. "So you ladies know Ranley?" said Mumford. "Then you know what a splendid fellow he is. He is like a brother to me."

"I should not like to give you the impression that we are well acquainted with Lord Ranley," said Verity. "We have had the pleasure of meeting him in London. I am certain he would have no recollection of Miss Reynolds and myself. He is such a famous man and meets so many people."

Mumford nodded. "Well, I cannot imagine him not remembering meeting such beautiful young ladies as yourselves. Ranley was not one to forget anything. Indeed, I never saw a man who could learn his lines with such ease. He could read his part once and commit it to memory." Mumford directed a significant glance at Von Hoffman. "Would that every actor could do as well. But then, Ranley was a remarkable man, utterly remarkable indeed. I am proud to claim him as a friend."

Finding discussion of Ranley strangely discomfiting, Verity was eager to change the subject. "Are you staying long in Cornwall, Mr. Mumford?"

"Three weeks. That is what we have planned, but, indeed, if the houses are not up to our expectations, we may depart earlier. Then on to the east. We are on a grand tour, you see. But I have talked on and on and you ladies have said so little. Are you traveling through Cornwall?"

"We are staying here for a time," said Verity. "We have just arrived. It is quite lovely here and I know we will like it very much."

"Are you not visiting relations or friends, ma'am?"

"No, we know no one. My late husband was from Cornwall, you see, but he had no relations left. I did want to see the places where my dear Oliver lived as a boy. It was not so very far from Truro."

"My deep condolences to you, Mrs. Trelawney," said Mumford.

"You are very kind, sir," said Verity. "I hope to find a small cottage where we can live economically. Miss Reynolds and I have few resources and must carefully husband them." She sighed rather melodramatically.

"But have you no one to assist you?" said Mumford.

Verity sighed again. "No one, sir. We are quite friendless. But I do not wish to convey the impression that we are utterly impoverished. No indeed, we have sufficient means to live modestly."

Mumford eyed Verity, thinking that she did not look to be the sort of young woman who had much experience with living modestly. He was somewhat puzzled by her and her companion. Mrs. Trelawney spoke like a lady of quality and had such an aristocratic bearing that one would have taken her for a member of society. Indeed, if she were not a member of the gentry or aristocracy, she was a very good actress. And although her companion was not so genteel, Mumford judged Miss Reynolds to be a pretty little minx.

An idea suddenly occurred to the theater company director, but he hesitated a moment before voicing it. "I pray you will forgive my impertinence, Mrs. Trelawney, but I have had a thought. It appears you are in somewhat straitened circumstances."

"Somewhat," said Verity, directing a curious look at Mumford.

"Have you ever considered appearing on the stage? Oh, it is quite bold of me to suggest it, but I do think you would be marvelous. And Miss Reynolds, too."

Nell regarded Mumford in astonishment. The gentleman was suggesting that Lady Verity de Lacy appear on the public stage like a common actress! It was utterly ridiculous. Nell turned to her mistress, expecting to see that young lady burst into gales of laughter at the preposterous idea. To her shock,

Nell found Verity looking completely serious. Nell suddenly had a sinking feeling.

"You see, Mrs. Trelawney," continued Mumford, "as I have said, our leading lady has left us in undue haste. And we are in need of another actress as well. Perhaps you ladies would consider the idea and give me your decision in the morning. While we are not rich, dear ladies, I can tell you that such a life as ours it not a bad living. No indeed, I expect we will do very well."

"You are very kind, Mr. Mumford," said Verity, "but you cannot have the least idea how Miss Reynolds and I would perform upon the stage. Although I will admit I have acted a little as an amateur."

"Aha!" said Mumford. "I knew it. And you were doubtlessly excellent. And what of you, Miss Reynolds? Have you acted as well?"

"No, sir," said Nell, "and I should make a muddle of it if I tried."

"Nonsense, Nell," said Verity. "I should think acting would suit you."

Nell did not like the direction the conversation was taking. She was alarmed that Verity did not reject Mumford's outrageous suggestion outright. The theater director continued to extoll the advantages of a career with his company and finally received Verity's promise to consider the matter. Nell was relieved when they said farewell to Mr. Mumford and his companions and retired to their rooms.

Once Nell had shut the door and was certain that they were alone, she implored her mistress, "Surely, my lady, you cannot be considering that you would become an actress."

Verity sat down upon the bed and felt the lumpy mattress. "Why, Nell, do not look so horrified. Indeed, it is not a bad idea."

"My lady! Oh, I know I should say Mrs. Trelawney, but I can hardly think of such things at a time like this. What would Lord Benbrook say if he knew that you were thinking of becoming an actress?"

"It should serve my father right for his infamous treatment of me," said Verity. "I do not care what he or anyone thinks of me. Why should I not become an actress? After all, it will not be Verity de Lacy on the stage. It will be poor Mrs. Trelawney. You cannot imagine that anyone I know would see me here in Cornwall. Yes, the more I consider the matter, the more I believe that I like it. And I have often thought that you would be excellent as an actress, Nell. Why, you read Princess Thalia so beautifully when I was writing *The Warrior Princess.*"

Nell looked thoughtful. She was not totally unsusceptible to the idea of becoming an actress herself. In fact, she had more than once thought of appearing on the stage. Surely it was not unusual that a young woman who loved the theater and who was now employed by an aspiring playwright had considered the idea. How many times had Nell daydreamed of exchanging her life in service for the glamorous albeit rather dangerous life of an actress? "I would be terrified to speak in front of anyone, my lady."

"Nonsense, Nell. I want you to think on the matter as I shall do tonight. We will discuss it in the morning."

"Very well . . . Mrs. Trelawney."

Verity smiled. "I did like Mr. Mumford. He was a most amiable gentleman."

"And did you not think Mr. Von Hoffman the most handsome man you have ever seen?"

"Nell," said Verity with mock sterness, "I was under the impression that you thought Lord Ranley was the most handsome man you had ever seen."

"Yes, I did think that," returned Nell, "but that was before I had seen Mr. Von Hoffman. What a pity that he is a foreign gentleman."

"He can not help that, Nell."

"I suppose not," said Nell wistfully as she began to assist her mistress to prepare for bed.

18

Baron Ranley eyed himself in the mirror as his valet brushed his coat to remove every bit of offending lint. Even the most critical of observers could not deny that his lordship looked handsome in his well-tailored coat, nankeen pantaloons, and gleaming boots. The baron nodded approvingly at his reflection, concluding that he looked appropriately stylish but not slavishly attentive to fashion.

"Thank you, Tucker. That will be all."

"Very good, my lord," said the servant, taking his leave.

Alone in the room, Ranley stared thoughtfully out the window. Things had been going extraordinarily well for him, he reflected. Hawkins had been ecstatic about his new play, which was now in rehearsal, and his revitalized interest in the theater had driven away the melancholy that had been plaguing him for some time.

The baron had cut down on his drinking and he had all but abandoned the ruinous gaming that Hawkins had continually warned him against. He had resumed his friendships with his old theatrical friends, finding himself happier in their company than in that of more aristocratic society. In short, Ranley was busy and, for the most part, content.

There was, however, one thing that prevented the baron from being entirely at peace. That was the problem of Verity de Lacy. His lordship had considered Verity something of a problem since he had first met her, for she had been in his thoughts much more frequently than he would have wished. He had tried to turn his attentions to one of the other ladies who were vying for his affections, but the picture of Verity de Lacy kept appearing to him with alarming persistence.

That she was missing from Society was entirely unsettling and Ranley spent much time in the two weeks that followed Benbrook's visit to him wondering where she might have gone and if she had returned. Since he had heard through the usual channels of gossip that Verity had gone to visit a cousin in Kent, he concluded that she had not returned.

Although he tried to tell himself that Verity's disappearance was of no consequence to him, Ranley grew worried as the days went on. As he stood in his bedchamber, looking out the window, he wondered if he should call at Benbrook House. He knew very well that Benbrook would not want to see him. Indeed, the earl would probably consider a visit from him unwelcome and impertinent.

Ranley pondered the matter for a time and then walked from the room. Arriving downstairs, he called for his carriage and directed the driver to take him to Benbrook House.

When he arrived there, the butler brought Ranley's card in to Lord and Lady Benbrook, who were engaged in serious discussion in the drawing room. The earl picked up the card. "Ranley," he said.

"Do you think he might have heard something about Verity?" said the countess.

"I doubt it," returned his lordship. "Yet I daresay we should receive him. He behaved very decently to me when I called on him."

"Then do show him in, Weeks," said Lady Benbrook, addressing the butler.

The man retreated, returning shortly with the baron. Ranley bowed to the countess and nodded to Benbrook. "I must ask you to forgive me for intruding, but I wondered if you had heard anything from Lady Verity. Oh, I know it is none of my concern, but since you visited me, sir, I confess I have been somewhat worried about the young lady."

"That is good of you, Ranley," returned the countess. She frowned and looked rather doleful. "Do sit down." When the gentlemen were seated, she resumed. "You are one of the few persons who knows what has happened. We were able to put a story about that Verity had gone to visit her cousin. Thank heaven everyone seems to accept it."

"We are searching everywhere," said the earl. "Discreetly, of course. And we have received a letter from her."

"A letter?" said Ranley, somewhat relieved.

"Yes," said the countess. "It was posted from London, but we are certain she is not in town. I daresay she had someone post it for her. She is dreadfully clever.

"But she assures us she is very well and that she has enough money to live on. Where she has gotten it is a mystery for she has taken none of her jewels and very few of her clothes. We are very worried, as you might imagine."

"When I see the chit again," said the earl, "I will not go easy on her."

"Oh, Benbrook," exclaimed the countess, "you must not speak in such an odious fashion. If I could but see my dearest Verity again, I should be the happiest woman in the kingdom. And what are we to tell her dear brothers? They have been staying with their cousins in Kent, but are to come home soon."

"I am so sorry," said Ranley, "but it is likely that Lady Verity will come to her senses and return."

"Come to her senses?" said Benbrook. "Hardly likely with that girl."

"Benbrook," said the countess reprovingly. She turned to the baron. "I do hope that will happen, Ranley."

"I hope so, too, Lady Benbrook," replied the baron. "If there is anything that I might do to assist you, I should be more than willing to do so."

"That is very good of you, sir," returned Benbrook, "but I can think of nothing anyone might do. Should you hear any word from her, I pray you will inform us."

"Indeed I shall, although upon my word, I should think it remarkable if Lady Verity would get in touch with me. Well, I shall take my leave." Ranley made his farewells and left the Benbrooks. He got into his carriage once more and proceeded to his club.

Returning home some time later, Ranley retreated to his library where he perused the morning post. There was a great many letters and the baron sifted through them. Thinking he recognized the handwriting of one missive, he opened it. "Yes, it is from Mumford, the old rascal," murmured the baron with a smile.

Josiah Mumford was well known to his lordship. He was one of many friends from the baron's early acting days. They had shared many adventures while touring with a rather disreputable troupe of actors. The baron remembered those days fondly despite the fact that they were hardly prosperous times for any of them.

The baron sat back, eager to read the letter. Mumford was a favorite of Ranley's despite or perhaps because of the fact that he was a verbose fellow, prone to hyperbole. He began his letter assuring the baron that he was doing very well indeed and that he had assembled the greatest group of players England had ever seen.

Ranley smiled as Mumford described the various members of his company, hinting that each one was far superior to anyone appearing on stage at the Queen's Theater. The baron continued reading, but stopped at one paragraph. "And, my dear Brutus, I cannot express my joy at the new actress who has joined the company. It was destiny finding this lady and a fair companion in the very inn where we were staying. She is a young widow named Mrs. Trelawney. I must tell you, my friend, that this lady combines the beauty of Helen with the wisdom of Athena. She has raven black hair and the most dazzling blue eyes. And what an actress she is! I have never seen her like in all of England. And truly, there is no one, save yourself, Brutus, who could learn a part so swiftly. Indeed, this lady is a marvel. Her companion, Miss Reynolds, is a delightful little fair-haired creature and she, too, has the makings of a fine actress. The ladies said they had met you in London. Doubtless you remember them.''

Ranley reread the paragraph twice. Mrs. Trelawney and Miss Reynolds? The baron's brow furrowed in concentration. ''Black hair and dazzling blue eyes?'' he muttered aloud. ''The beauty of Helen combined with the wisdom of Athena? He goes a trifle far, but by God, this could very well be Verity de Lacy and her faithful Nell.''

The baron hurriedly read the rest of the letter in which Mumford told of his company's itinerary. So they would be in Truro for another week, he told himself. Ranley's days as a traveling player had made him well acquainted with the kingdom's geography. There were scarcely any parts of the far-flung provinces that he had not visited.

So Verity was in Cornwall, he mused. Or perhaps this Mrs. Trelawney was not Verity. Certainly she was not the only black-haired girl with a talent for acting in all of England. Ranley frowned and rose from his chair. After pacing across the library, he stopped and considered the matter. He could return to Benbrook House and tell the earl of his suspicions.

After considering the idea, the baron rejected it. Benbrook would be furious at the idea that his daughter would appear on the stage. And if the lady were not Verity, the baron reasoned that he would have caused undue distress to both Lord and Lady Benbrook. Still, Ranley had a strong feeling that he was right. Indeed, joining a theater company was just the sort of thing a headstrong female like Verity de Lacy would do.

There was only one course of action to take, concluded Ranley. He would go to Cornwall himself and find Verity. He would attempt to talk some sense into her and see that she returned to London.

It had been many years since the baron had been to Cornwall and his experiences there had not made him eager to return. Still, for some reason, he felt it was his duty to involve himself in the matter. Why, he could not say, but that did not seem to signify. A resolute look upon his face, the baron rang for a servant and commanded the surprised footman that he wished his traveling carriage to be made ready at once.

19

Ranley sat in his carriage studying the flat moorland he was passing through. The sky was dark and threatening and the scenery looked dreary. As the conveyance hit another of the innumerable bumps and potholes on this stretch of desolate road, the baron muttered a curse and wondered what had got into him to set off on such a journey.

He had been two days traveling and had spent two nights in inns. Although the accommodations were certainly not the worst he had ever seen, Ranley found himself missing his comfortable bed, excellent table, and the familiar servants who catered to his every want. He had grown soft with luxury, he told himself disapprovingly, but indeed, he had and could not deny it.

The journey seemed interminable. Ranley was bored, with no one with whom to converse and so little interesting scenery to provide diversion. His mind could not help but wander, not an unusual or undesirable circumstance for a playwright, perhaps. But Ranley's mind was not wandering to ideas for new plays. Instead, he seemed able to focus on one thing alone and that was Verity de Lacy.

As the carriage lumbered on, the baron's reflections were interrupted suddenly and dramatically. There was a cracking sound and then a great jolt as the vehicle lurched to a stop and Ranley was thrown forward into the opposite seat. "What in God's name has happened, Burke?" cried the baron, opening the door of the carriage.

"I am sorry, my lord," said the driver, hurrying to put down the steps so Ranley could alight. "It is the wheel, my lord. Completely broken."

"Dammit!" cried the baron. "Broken here in this godforsaken place?"

"It is very bad, my lord."

The groom, who had been studying the broken wheel, joined them. "We'll get no farther today, my lord," he said. "But there is a village just up ahead."

"There is?" said Ranley looking down the road. A mist obscured the view, but it did appear that there was a village a short distance from them. He could see light as if from a lantern. "Thank God," said the baron. "Then we'll be able to get assistance."

"Aye, I do hope so, my lord," said the driver. The servants managed to get the disabled vehicle to the side of the road and then the groom unhitched the horses. It was decided that Ranley and the driver would take the horses to the village, leaving the groom to guard the carriage.

Although it was not a very large village, the baron was grateful that a settlement of any kind existed so close to their unfortunate mishap. As they entered the village Ranley reminded the driver to address him as "Mr. Thompson." The baron often used this or some other suitably nondescript name when traveling, for his fame was such that he got little peace when strangers knew that the reknowned Lord Brutus Ranley was among them.

The local inhabitants seemed sympathetic to their plight and Ranley was reassured to hear that there was a fine wheelwright in the village. The rub, however, was that the wheel-right was at present visiting his sister in Truro, but he would be back late that afternoon or early in the evening.

The baron greeted this information with admirable equanimity. "How far is it to Truro?" he asked.

"Six, nearly seven miles," replied one of the local men.

"So close as that?" said Ranley. He considered the situation. "Burke," he said, addressing the driver, "I should like to get to Truro today. You and Edward can wait here and see to the carriage. I'll go on and you can join me in Truro when the carriage is fixed." He turned to the local man. "I should like to hire a horse."

"Sorry, sir, but none be here to hire. And there be no one to take you. But it be not a bad walk in such fine weather as this."

Ranley was not sure whether the man was quizzing him, for a fine mist was falling and the sky looked like it could grow much worse. "I shall walk then. I would be there by mid afternoon."

"Would you not want Edward to go with you, Mr. Thompson?" said the driver, addressing the baron.

"No, Burke, I shall go alone. When I arrive in Truro I shall take a room somewhere." Ranley looked at the local man. "Is there a good inn or hotel in Truro?"

"Aye, sir, the Black Swan. 'Tis a nice respectable inn."

"Then that's where I'll be, Burke."

After a few more instructions to his servant, Ranley set out down the road. Despite the mist, it was not a bad day for walking. As he strode along, the baron was glad to be out of the carriage with the chance to stretch his legs.

However, after an hour and a half, his lordship found himself thinking fondly of the plush upholstery of his carriage. He was beginning to grow a bit footsore, and the mist had changed to a drizzle. There was little sign of life along the road and the dreary gray weather made the landscape seem bleak and uninteresting.

The road turned ahead at a group of trees and as Ranley

came up to the bend in the road, he was startled at the sudden appearance of a man from the thicket. "Good day to you, sir," he said.

"Good day," returned Ranley, taking in the man's appearance. Tall and broad-shouldered, the man was dressed in a cloak and wide-brimmed hat. He had a very noticeable scar on his cheek and when he smiled, the baron noted he was missing one of his front teeth.

"Not many gentlemen to be found walking this road," said the stranger. "Bound for Truro, are you, sir?"

Ranley nodded. "Is it much farther?"

"Nay, but two miles ahead."

"Good," said Ranley. He nodded to the man and started to resume walking, but the stranger stopped in front of him, blocking his departure.

"Before you are off, sir, I should be obliged if you would favor me with your money."

The baron regarded him in astonishment. "Stand aside," he said.

The man smiled. Then pulling out a pistol from beneath his cloak, he pointed it at the baron. "Your money or your life. It is your choice, sir."

"You are a damned footpad," said Ranley. "You cannot think you will get away with this."

"Why, indeed I do, sir," returned the robber. "Indeed I do. Now will you be so good as to hand me your blunt, or must I ruin your fine coat by putting a ball through it?"

For a brief moment Ranley considered the idea of trying to overpower the footpad. Yet the baron wisely rejected such rash behavior. "Very well, you damned villain." He handed over his purse.

The robber weighed the leather bag in his hand. "Very good, sir. It appears I've plucked a fat partridge indeed. Now your watch, sir."

Ranley scowled at the man, but obediently gave up his watch.

"And your hat and coat."

"You go too far, man," said the baron hotly.

"Quiet or I'll have your boots as well."

His lordship again thought of putting up a fight, but reason prevailed. He took off his fine beaver hat and tossed it to the bandit, who took off his own and tried on Ranley's. "Why, it fits very well, don't you think, sir? Now your coat." Ranley glared at the man, but took off his well-tailored garment. "Why, 'tis a very fine coat, this," said the robber, taking the coat from the baron. "And to show that I am not a bad fellow, I shall give you my hat." He threw his battered, broad-brimmed hat on the ground in front of the baron. "And now you may be on your way, sir. I thank you very kindly."

"You impudent scoundrel," said Ranley, clenching his fists. "I'll see you hang."

"Oh, I doubt that, sir," returned the footpad. "Good day to you then." With those words he retreated into the trees and was gone.

Ranley cursed angrily, but realized that there was nothing he could do. Since the drizzle was still falling, he picked up the robber's wretched hat and reluctantly placed it upon his head. He then started walking toward Truro once again.

The baron considered it a most fortuitous circumstance that he arrived at the town just as the rain began to fall in earnest. The sign of the Black Swan Inn was one of the first things Ranley noticed as he entered Truro. He hurried inside to get out of the rain.

"Raining cats and dogs, eh, sir?" said the proprietor, eyeing the baron with interest.

Ranley took off the robber's hat and nodded to the innkeeper. "Where might I find the constable? I have been robbed."

"You don't say, sir," said the innkeeper. "Did he take your coat, sir?"

The baron found the question irritating. "He did indeed. And my purse, my watch, and a beaver hat I paid a damned high price for not three weeks ago."

"This is quite dreadful," said the innkeeper. "You must

go sit by the fire, sir. I'll send a lad for the constable. You must have a pint, sir. You will feel much better.''

Ranley did feel somewhat better once he was seated before the fire with a pint of ale in his hand. The proprietor was an excellent, hospitable fellow who had quickly dispatched a boy to bring back the constable. This was soon done and the police officer listened with keen interest to the baron's tale. After hearing Ranley's description of the robber, the constable pronounced the unfortunate episode just one more in a great string of crimes perpetrated by one Bob Tully. The footpad was well known to everyone and, the constable assured Ranley, he would be brought to justice soon.

The baron was not so certain of this, but he appreciated the constable's concern and the innkeeper's sympathy. When they had left him, he settled back in his chair and stared into the fire. Well, he was in Truro, he told himself, and perhaps here he would find Verity de Lacy. He frowned. Or perhaps she would not be here and he had come all this way for nothing. The idea did not please the baron and he decided that he would immediately seek out Josiah Mumford and his band of players.

Scarcely had he had this thought when he caught sight of a young woman walking across the public room of the inn. He recognized her at once as Nell Dawson. Leaping to his feet, Ranley hurried after Nell, who had walked briskly from the public room and up the stairway that led to the guests' rooms. Following her up the stairs, the baron caught up with Nell as she paused in front of the door to her rooms.

''Miss Dawson!''

Nell spun around, astonished to hear her name. Her eyes opened wide in shock as she recognized the baron. ''My lord!''

''Where is Lady Verity?'' demanded Ranley. ''Is she here?'' Nell shook her head. ''Then where is she?'' When Nell hesitated, he continued. ''You may tell me. Indeed, I know all about Mrs. Trelawney and Miss Reynolds and your misguided careers as actresses.''

"But how could you?" said Nell.

"That does not signify, Miss Reynolds. Now where is she?"

"At rehearsal, my lord. But however did you find us? Does Lord Benbrook know where her ladyship is?"

"No, he does not. But, indeed, he will know soon enough. Now you will take me to your mistress at once."

Nell nodded reluctantly. "But I must first fetch her ladyship's cloak."

Ranley nodded. "Be quick about it then."

When Nell had retrieved the cloak, she led Ranley from the inn out into the rainy streets of Truro. It was only a short way to the hall where the rehearsal of the theater troupe was now in progress. They entered through a back door and made their way to the side of the stage.

Mumford's company was in dress rehearsal. The baron did not recognize the play. There was a dreadful lot of clamor and movement on stage with little intelligible dialogue. Ranley watched a massive blond fellow in what appeared to be a pirate's garb move to center stage to speak his lines. The man spoke with histrionic abandon in a pronounced German accent that caused Ranley to nearly burst into laughter.

Verity appeared on stage at that moment. Dressed like a medieval princess and wearing a glittering tiara on her head, she walked regally across the stage. Ranley found his eyes glued to her as she began to speak. "My faithful friend," said Verity serenely, "what gladness greets your appearance. Prince Odo has by insidious enemies been imprisoned. What fate meets my lord, I know not and I despair!"

"Knaves and villains!" cried the blond man passionately. "The prince is taken! But fear not, fair princess, by my strong arm shall he be freed!"

Ranley could not prevent a laugh from escaping his lips at the fevered way in which that line was delivered. Nell regarded him with disapproval. "You must be quiet, my lord," she whispered.

"I am sorry," replied the baron in a low voice. "And do not call me 'my lord.' I am Mr. Thompson at present."

Nell frowned. So now Lord Ranley was Mr. Thompson just as Lady Verity was Mrs. Trelawney. It was confusing and somewhat annoying.

The play continued and Ranley did his best to keep his composure. He found the drama quite funny and absurd, although it was intended to be completely serious. Verity, he noted, was the only player who was not totally preposterous. Indeed, she was excellent, shining out like a candle in the fog.

Ranley looked out from the wings into the hall where benches filled a large room. Seated there was his old friend Mumford. The baron smiled as he recognized his old comrade. Mumford was little changed, but for the fact he had grown somewhat stouter. He was watching the rehearsal with a decidedly unhappy look.

Proceeding to stage left, Verity glanced over into the wings. Then she caught sight of the baron. Verity's astonishment was only briefly visible on her face. Like a seasoned trouper, she continued with her part, not allowing the startling appearance of Ranley to rattle her. After making an impassioned speech, she made her exit, leaving her fellow actor Von Hoffman alone to deliver a lengthy soliloquy. Once off stage she hurried toward the baron. "What are you doing here?" she whispered.

"My dear Mrs. Trelawney," said Ranley with an exaggerated bow, "how good it is to see you again."

"What are you doing here, Ranley?" she whispered again.

"What would I be doing here? I have come to find you."

"To find me? How did you know where I am? Does anyone else know?"

"No one. I had a letter from Mumford. He is an old friend of mine. I thought Mrs. Trelawney and Miss Reynolds sounded very familiar."

Verity looked very much relieved. "Then my father does not know where I am? Thank heaven for that."

"And, although you apparently do not care in the least, I must tell you that your parents are very worried about you."

"Of course, I care," said Verity indignantly. "I have written them that I am well. And if I may say so, Ranley, this is no affair of yours."

"It is Mr. Thompson," interjected Nell. "His lordship wants to be called Mr. Thompson."

"Does he indeed?" returned Verity. "So you are incognito, sir?"

"I think it best to remain so."

"Oh, due to your great fame I suppose," said Verity sarcastically.

"Indeed so," returned the baron in some irritation.

"I have no time to say any more, Mr. Thompson. I must go. I have another scene." She hurried away, vanishing behind the curtains.

The play continued. It was in its final act, which Ranley considered a mercy. It was a dreadful play and without Verity's performance, it would have been a total disaster. When it was over, the players stood expectantly before Mumford.

"It will have to do, I suppose," said that gentleman. "Yes, we have no time for changes. Do go on, all of you. You'll need some rest before tonight." The troupe was somewhat disheartened by its leader's comments.

Verity hurried back to where Ranley and Nell were standing. "Did you think it was dreadful?"

The baron shrugged. "You were excellent, Mrs. Trelawney. I cannot say the same for your colleagues. That German fellow for instance. Good God!"

"Mr. Von Hoffman is a wonderful gentleman," said Nell indignantly.

"Yes, he is a kind and considerate man," said Verity.

"I should not doubt that he has the most sterling character imaginable, but his acting was appalling."

"I should advise you, Mr. Thompson," said Verity severely, "to keep your criticisms to yourself. We will learn soon enough what an audience thinks of the performance.''

"That is what I fear,'' returned the baron. "I am all too familiar with the reactions of the provincial mob. I have had my share of foul-smelling eggs pelted at me.''

"You have?'' said Verity, genuinely surprised.

"It was some time ago,'' said Ranley with a smile. "Now I must go and greet Mumford, but I have much more to say to you, Mrs. Trelawney.''

Verity frowned at this remark, but made no reply as the baron hurried toward Mumford. The manager of the theater company had seated himself back on a bench in the empty hall. He sat glumly, his head cradled in his hands. Ranley walked out onto the stage. "A horse! A horse!'' he shouted. "My kingdom for a horse!''

Mumford's head shot up and he grinned in amazement. "My dear friend, can it be you?''

Ranley jumped down from the steps and rushed to embrace Mumford, who burst into tears of joy. "Mumford, old fellow,'' said the baron, extricating himself from his friend's embrace. "How good it is to see you!''

"I cannot believe this!'' said Mumford. "Brutus Ranley here in Cornwall! It cannot be possible!''

"It is indeed possible, for here I am, but, my dear Mumford, I should prefer it if no one knew who I am.''

"Oh,'' said the theater manager. "But if everyone knew you were here to see my play, I should think I should sell a good many more tickets.''

"Please, Mumford, do indulge me in this.''

"Very well, Brutus. I quite understand.''

"I am calling myself Thompson,'' said the baron.

"Thompson,'' repeated Mumford. "Very well.'' He suddenly noticed that the baron was dressed in his waistcoat and shirtsleeves. "Is something amiss, my dear boy? This is not the sartorial splendor I remember from you.''

Ranley laughed. "I was robbed by a footpad who took my coat and hat.''

"Damnation!'' cried Mumford.

"Took your hat?" Verity's voice entered the conversation. She and Nell had given Ranley a few moments for their reunion and then had joined them.

"Yes, and a goodly sum in gold sovereigns. And this happened after my carriage broke down. I walked seven miles here. As you can imagine, I was not in the best of moods when I arrived at Truro."

"We will find you a coat at once," said Mumford. "My dear boy Harold has one that will fit you. Oh, my dear friend, you will not believe how Harold has grown."

"I daresay he has grown a good deal since he was scarcely seven years old when last I saw him."

"It has been such a long time. Why, I still cannot believe that you are here."

"After reading your letter, Mumford, I had a strange desire to see your company." He directed a meaningful look at Verity. "You spoke so well of Mrs. Trelawney here."

"Yes, yes, she is quite remarkable," said Mumford. "You did remember the ladies then?"

"Indeed I did. They are quite memorable."

"I am so very flattered that his lordship remembered us," said Verity with a mischievous smile. "I could not have expected him to do so."

"The memory of an elephant, Mrs. Trelawney," said the baron, tapping a forefinger to the side of his head. "I recollect even the most insignificant things."

"I have reason to know about your memory, sir," returned Verity.

This remark caused Mumford to regard his old friend and new leading lady with interest, but no further explanation was forthcoming. "Brutus, do say you are staying in Truro for a time."

"For a time, Mumford."

"Good. I shall be eager to see what you think of the performance tonight. Did you see *The Revenge of Prince Odo*? What did you think?"

"I saw but a small portion of it," said Ranley guardedly.

"I hesitate to reach an opinion based on seeing so little. I will say that Mrs. Trelawney was quite good."

"Yes, yes," said Mumford. "She is a marvel. Miss Reynolds is excellent as well. You will see her as the nurse in *Romeo and Juliet*. Yes, we have a fine program this evening. There is a brief comedy called *The Duke's Disappointment,* then *The Revenge of Prince Odo,* and finally *Romeo and Juliet.* Miss Pettigrew will dance the hornpipe in between."

"It sounds splendid," said Ranley.

"Oh, indeed it is. Now why don't we all have tea? Yes, that is a capital idea. We can meet at the Black Swan. I will fetch that coat for you, too, my dear Ranley—that is, Thompson."

Verity and Nell left the gentlemen to go to the crowded makeshift dressing room where Verity could change from her costume. "I thought I might faint when I saw Mr. Thompson," said Nell, carefully taking off Verity's tiara. "Can you imagine his lordship being robbed by a footpad?"

"I suppose I must feel sorry for him," said Verity with studied indifference. "Why, he might have been killed. But I cannot imagine why he felt compelled to come here," said Verity. "It is very odd."

"Yes, ma'am," returned Nell thoughtfully. An insightful young woman, Nell had been pondering the baron's sudden appearance. Her conclusion was unmistakeable—that Ranley was in love with Verity. However, Nell discreetly refrained from telling her mistress this theory.

"And now he will watch us tonight," said Verity. "I am so nervous already. I scarcely needed the great Ranley in the audience watching my every move. He is probably a harsh critic."

"I fear so, ma'am. Did you hear those terrible things he said about Mr. Von Hoffman?"

"Yes, I did, Nell, but we must not worry about Mr. Thompson. We must pretend that he is not here." However, knowing how much her thoughts alighted on Ranley's good-looking countenance even when he was in London, Verity knew very well that her words were ridiculous.

Most of the members of the troupe assembled in the Black Swan for refreshment and fellowship. Although the actors had been performing for a fortnight in Truro, that evening marked the opening of their new program. They had worked hard to publicize the event, and they had reason to believe that a very respectable crowd would come to mark the great occasion.

Ranley, now dressed in Harold's ill-fitting brown coat, was extremely cheerful. He was charming to all the company, none of whom seemed to know who he actually was. Mumford introduced him as an old friend and former actor. Knowing that the newcomer was a member of their acting fraternity, all the members of the company were friendly and welcoming.

Verity watched the baron with amused interest. She had not expected him to shine in such humble circumstances, but then she reminded herself, he was not unaccustomed to this sort of life and company. Verity was glad that Ranley seemed to be enjoying himself so much. She expected his censure, but was happy that circumstances prevented him for the time being from lecturing her about returning to town.

Verity was enjoying herself immensely. She reflected as she ate a piece of bread and butter that she had never been happier in her life than she was now in Cornwall. Joining the theatrical troupe had been the most exciting thing she had ever done. She took to acting like a duck to water and she knew that she was very good. Verity loved everyone in the troupe and everyone loved her, even Miss Pettigrew, who might have been expected to be jealous since Verity had taken on roles she might have had. Yet Miss Pettigrew was a dear friend already. Yes, Verity liked being an actress and only wished that life could go on like this for some time.

Harold Mumford, on the other hand was looking very glum as he sat beside his father at the table. Sitting in silence for a long time, he seemed to be debating with himself about what to say. "Father," he said finally, tugging at Mumford's sleeve, "might I have a word?"

"What is it, dear lad?" said Mumford.

Harold spoke in a low voice. The others at the table could not hear what he said and they continued to chat. Verity was across the table from Ranley, but she did not exchange much conversation with him. Miss Pettigrew was on one side of the baron and Mumford on the other. Since both of them were talkative individuals, they kept Ranley occupied.

Verity found herself in the role of observer. She sat next to Von Hoffman, but that gentleman was more interested in Nell, who sat on his other side and hung upon his every word. Verity noted young Harold's troubled expression and Mumford's sudden look of incredulity. "You cannot be serious, Harry!"

"But I am, Father. I cannot do it. I was mad to think I could. I shall be laughed out of the hall."

These words were spoken in a louder voice and everyone at the table turned to regard Harold and Mumford. "My friends," said the theater company director, "I fear Harold has said he does not wish to go on as Romeo."

"What!" cried Miss Pettigrew. "But you must, Harold!"

"Indeed so," said Von Hoffman. "There is no one else to do so."

"I cannot do it!" cried Harold, now quite distraught. "You all know I cannot do it. I have not had enough practice! Oh, why did Mr. Willison have to run off the way he did? I am no Romeo."

"Harold," said Mumford sternly. "There are scarcely two hours before the performance. There is no one else who knows the part—except myself of course."

"Then you can do it, Father," cried Harold.

"I? Why I would appear ridiculous. No, you will do it, my lad, or you will rue the day you were ever born."

This uncompromising remark caused Harold to bury his head in his hands and burst into sobs.

"Good God!" said Mumford. "Take hold of yourself, boy."

"Mr. Mumford," cried Verity, filled with sympathy for the young man. "Harold is in great distress. It is a very difficult part for him."

"Yes, yes," said Mumford. "But he will have to do it. There is no alternative."

Verity frowned and then an idea struck her. "But Mr. Mumford, there is an alternative. Mr. Thompson can play Romeo."

"What!" cried Ranley looking at her in horror.

"Yes, of course," said Verity. "He knows the part. You know that he is a quite passable actor, don't you, Mr. Mumford?"

Mumford grinned. "Indeed he is. What say you, Bru—that is, Thompson? Come, say you will do it."

"I will not," said Ranley firmly. "Nothing can persuade me. I am no longer an actor."

"Once an actor, always an actor," returned Mumford. "I pray you have some sympathy for my poor boy here. And it is but a small favor, my dear Thompson. Why, you and Mrs. Trelawney will be marvelous. Say you will do it. You will have my undying gratitude."

Ranley frowned over at Verity, who only smiled brightly at him. "Very well," he said reluctantly. Harold raised his head and grinned while his father pumped the baron's hand vigorously. Ranley frowned again at Verity, but that young lady only laughed delightedly.

20

A large group of people assembled in the hall, eager for diversion. Since placards had been plastered all throughout the town and surrounding villages, there were few in the area who were unaware that Mumford's renowned players were performing an all new program that evening. Indeed, as the playbills dramatically announced, Truro was about to witness a never before performed masterpiece entitled *The Revenge of Prince Odo*. The advertisement stated that since this great work had never been seen on the London stage, the residents of the area should consider themselves very fortunate indeed.

Mumford was very excited that his advertisements had had the hoped-for effect. It was a very large crowd, even larger than he had expected. Since all of the persons now filling the hall had paid two shillings for the privilege of viewing the night's entertainment, Mumford knew he would do extremely well that night. The theater company director had additional cause for joy for among his players was the renowned Brutus Ranley. Whatever doubts he might have had about the competence of certain players of his company, they were entirely swept aside by the baron's participation that evening.

Although it nearly broke his heart that he could not trumpet Ranley's presence to the world, Mumford was resigned to the baron's anonymity. He could very well understand that his old friend could scarcely be expected to appear on stage now that he was a peer of the realm. Indeed, it would be a great scandal if London Society got wind of it. Still, it was a very great secret for Mumford to keep and he was not a man accustomed to keeping secrets.

Although Ranley had immediately regretted so rashly agreeing to play Romeo, there was nothing he could do to extricate himself from the situation. After all, he had said he would do it, so he was condemned to go through with it. It was not that he doubted his ability to play the role, for he had played Romeo so many times in those now rather distant bygone days that it still seemed second nature. No, there was a general uneasiness about returning to the stage. It was, feared the baron, a part of his past that should remain in the past.

Mumford had shortened the play a good deal, cutting what he considered to be unnecessary scenes and speeches. In looking over the truncated play, Ranley had wondered if it would make sense to anyone, but Mumford had assured him that no one would mind in the least. Although the baron had wondered what he had gotten himself into, he made no complaint.

As he sat in the cluttered dressing room with the other actors, a flood of nostalgia passed over his lordship. It had been a very long time since he had applied his stage make-up and dressed in a costume. Karl Von Hoffman sat beside him, busily applying dark paint to his pale eyebrows. "So you have acted before, Thompson?" he said glancing over at the baron.

"I have some slight experience," said Ranley.

"I would hope you do not blunder," returned the German. "The reputation of the company is at stake."

The baron would have been annoyed at the remark if it did not strike him as so totally ludicrous. "I shall do my very best, Von Hoffman, but you cannot hold me to your high standards."

"You are perhaps right," said Von Hoffman, apparently oblivious to Ranley's sarcasm. "I must go. It is nearly time for starting."

Ranley watched the big German get up and leave the dressing room. He was attired in a heavy greatcoat. He wore high boots that came above his knees, an elaborate periwig, and the sort of enormous plumed hat worn by a buccaneer. The baron thought he looked ridiculous and wondered why the man always seemed to look like a pirate.

Wearing his Romeo costume, Ranley left the dressing room and proceeded to the area off stage where he intended to watch the performance. Since Mumford had scheduled *Romeo and Juliet* as the final play, the baron would have quite a lot of time before appearing himself.

There was a great deal of noise coming from the hall when Ranley took his place in the wings. Peering from behind the curtain, the baron saw that the benches were packed with an assortment of people of all ranks and stations. They talked noisily, laughing and calling to their friends and acquaintances across the hall.

The baron seemed pleased at finding what seemed to be an amiable audience. He scanned the crowd for ruffians and drunkards, but found none. That was a good sign, for his lordship was very familiar with the sort of rustic fellows who attended plays solely for the purpose of heaving large amounts of rotten vegetables at the actors.

No, concluded Ranley, it seemed a pleasant enough group. "What do you think, Mr. Thompson? A good house?"

The baron turned to find Verity standing beside him dressed in an elaborate costume. "Ah, Mrs. Trelawney. How beautiful you look."

Since Verity was uncertain whether Ranley was serious with this remark, she was not sure as to how to respond. "Thank you," she said finally.

Verity's costume was a late seventeenth century style gown of wine-colored satin with a wide skirt and low-cut bodice. She wore a curly red wig and large plumed hat. Ranley thought she looked stunning. "I hope you have a very large part and will appear on stage a good deal in this play, Mrs. Trelawney. No one will be able to take his eyes off you. The audience will, I hope, not notice Von Hoffman."

Verity was somewhat taken aback by this unexpected flattery, but she responded nonchalantly. "You are too hard on Mr. Von Hoffman."

"Am I? Why, the fellow had the audacity to tell me he hoped I would not 'blunder.' He fears that my performance will ruin everything."

"Oh, that is too funny," said Verity, laughing into her fan. "You must not take him too seriously. He is very nervous."

"And are you nervous, Mrs. Trelawney?"

"Why, I am terrified. We have not done any of these plays before—not before an audience, that is to say. I may make a great cake of myself."

"Nonsense," said the baron, "you will do splendidly. Now I shall be the one to make a great cake of himself."

"You, sir, are always wonderful. On stage, of course."

Ranley laughed. "I suppose that is a great compliment."

"It is indeed," said Verity, looking up into the baron's smiling countenance and feeling very much under his spell. "Oh, it will start soon." The small orchestra that was seated before the stage began to play a loud fanfare and Verity hurried to take her place on stage just as the curtain began to rise.

The Duke's Disappointment was a broad farce that involved numerous cases of mistaken identity, several outrageous coincidences, and an untold number of puns and pratfalls. It was exactly the sort of thing one might have expected the audience to love. While both Mumford and Verity performed very competently in their respective roles as an absent-minded duke and his prospective bride, the other actors performed dismally, a fact that the audience clearly resented.

Von Hoffman was particularly awful as Verity's other suitor. For some reason most everyone in the audience seemed to have taken a distinct dislike to him. Each time he spoke, he was greeted with catcalls and shouts of derision. Von Hoffman, for his part, responded to the theatergoers' displeasure with scowls and muffled German epithets, which delighted his antagonists and urged them on.

Ranley, watching from the side, realized that he had missed noting a group of particularly vociferous young gentlemen who had doubtlessly been drinking. The baron was glad that the young gentlemen's censure was confined to verbal assaults, but he wondered if such unruly behavior might dampen Verity's enthusiasm for the stage.

Yet fortunately the crowd's disfavor clearly did not include the lovely Mrs. Trelawney, for she was roundly cheered whenever she appeared. At the conclusion of the play, the audience loudly applauded Verity, but the shouts of a great number of rude persons made it clear that *The Duke's Disappointment* was not to their liking.

Miss Pettigrew then had the unenviable task of going before the increasingly hostile assembly to perform. Yet as the orchestra began to play the hornpipe, the audience was lifted from its sullen mood. While Miss Pettigrew was not necessarily the most talented of dancers, her efforts were applauded heartily. At the conclusion of the lively dance, Miss Pettigrew sang "Heart of Oak," an extremely popular choice, and everyone cheered her lustily.

This apparent change of mood of the audience encouraged Mumford, who was quite disturbed at the reception of his first offering. "I cannot understand it," he said, pausing briefly before Ranley. "They are unaccountably out for blood. I do feel it, Brutus. Well, I do think that *Prince Odo's Revenge* will make them come around."

"I do hope so," said the baron, suppressing a smile.

Despite Ranley's hopes, it was clear from the first line of *Prince Odo's Revenge* that the audience was prepared to detest it. The group of young gentlemen shouted their disapproval at everything save Verity's infrequent appearances, which they seemed to love. Von Hoffman's efforts brought nothing but laughter from the crowd, while poor Harold Mumford was quite disconcerted by the heckling he received in a mercifully brief role.

By the second act, things had gotten so disordered that Mumford appeared on stage to plead with the audience to behave. He was pelted with oranges for his efforts and forced off. "What am I to do?" cried Mumford hurrying to Ranley. "Do I dare go on with the second act?"

"I should think that might lead to an insurrection, my dear Mumford," said the baron. "Perhaps Miss Pettigrew might do another hornpipe. That seems to have a soothing effect."

"Perhaps you are right, dear Brutus," said Mumford.

Miss Pettigrew was none too eager to confront the audience again, but after Mumford's pleas, she gamely returned on stage. The crowd erupted into a roar of approval, much to Miss Pettigrew's great relief. The orchestra began to play and she began to dance to the great satisfaction of those assembled there.

Verity, who was now dressed in her princess costume, came to Mumford's side. "Oh, dear, Mr. Mumford, they quite hated *Prince Odo*. What are we to do?" She turned to the baron. "What do you think, Mr. Thompson?"

His lordship shrugged. "I might suggest concluding the performance early, although that may result in a demand for a refund of the ticket price on the part of a number of these ungrateful wretches."

"Indeed so," said Mumford. "We must not allow that or I am ruined."

"Then why don't we do *Romeo and Juliet*?" said Verity. "They can scarcely hate that more than they did *Prince Odo*."

"What do you think, Brutus?" said Mumford uneasily.

Ranley looked at Verity for a moment. Then he grinned. "Lay on Macduff!" he cried. "And damned be him that first cries, 'hold enough!' "

Taking this for assent, Mumford asked Verity to inform the cast members of the change and to hurry with her costume. She smiled at Ranley and rushed off.

By the time Miss Pettigrew had danced the hornpipe several times, the crowd was growing restless. She looked rather desperately toward Mumford in the wings, who signaled her to finish. She quickly concluded, curtsied, and made a hasty exit.

Mumford then proceeded bravely onto the stage. Ignoring the hoots of the troublesome young gentlemen, he announced the next offering. Then he quickly proceeded to set the stage for the bard's great tragedy. The opening scene was shortened, allowing Romeo to appear immediately.

The rude youths were rather surprised to find an actor appear whom they had not yet seen. They hesitated, vegetables in hand, while the ladies in the audience eyed the handsome newcomer with approval. Ranley strode to center stage accompanied by a rather flustered Harold Mumford, who had taken the lesser part of Romeo's cousin, Benvolio.

Ranley's first words transfixed the unruly audience. His melodious voice filled the hall, causing the youths to place their vegetables back into the sacks they had brought along. The baron, well aware of the effect his presence was exerting on his listeners, had a great feeling of power. As he continued, he knew that he had the audience in the palm of his hand. Even Von Hoffman's entrance as Mercutio did not break the hold he had on them. The audience seemed quite willing to suffer the German's abominable delivery of his lines in anticipation of Ranley's next words.

Verity had never seen anything like it before. She was strangely serene as she appeared in her first scene with Nell as the nurse and Miss Pettigrew as Juliet's mother. It all went very well and the audience applauded loudly.

Yet it was the first scene with both Romeo and Juliet that brought an unusual and respectful silence to the assembly. There was an unmistakeable electricity between Romeo and Juliet, apparent to all the delighted onlookers. It was not unnoticed by Ranley and Verity themselves as they spoke their lines, and gazed into each other's eyes. When they kissed, the audience cheered.

By the time that Juliet awakened to find her beloved Romeo dead, the members of the audience were wiping tears from their eyes. When Verity plunged the dagger into her breast, there was a collective gasp from the crowd and then sobs from both men and women as Juliet expired. Even the roughest of the young gentlemen had tears streaming down their cheeks.

When the play was over and Ranley and Verity rose up to take their bows, there was thunderous cheering. The baron looked over at Verity and took her hand. He led her forward and they bowed to the audience.

As Ranley surveyed the crowd, he smiled, realizing that in all his many triumphs on the stage, this performance in a rude hall in Cornwall was perhaps his best. Verity, flushed with pleasure and excitement, smiled at the audience. Then she looked over at Ranley and smiled brightly at her Romeo.

21

After the night's work, an ecstatic Mumford invited all of the company to the Black Swan for supper and celebration. It was some time before the actors were changed and able to make their way to the inn. Ranley and Verity were even longer delayed, having been detained by a number of admirers who insisted on offering their congratulations.

Among them were Mr. and Mrs. Baldwin, whom Verity had met on the Truro stagecoach. Although Mrs. Baldwin had been quite shocked to find Verity working as an actress, she had enjoyed the performance immensely. She and her husband were lavish in their praises of Verity's efforts, assuring her that she would doubtlessly have a sterling career. Mrs. Baldwin was even so bold as to invite Verity to call upon them, even though she thought the idea of receiving an actress in her home rather daring.

The baron, too, had his share of well-wishers. One middle-aged lady accompanied by her dour husband gushed that Ranley was the greatest actor she had ever seen. Confiding that she had twice had the pleasure of viewing the great

Brutus Ranley on the stage, she pronounced Mr. Thompson a much better actor and decidedly more handsome. The baron accepted this compliment with an amused smile.

When the last members of the audience took their leave, Ranley left the hall. He found Verity, Nell, and Von Hoffman standing in the street. "There you are, Mr. Thompson," said Verity. "I thought your admirers would never allow you to escape. We waited for you. It seemed only fitting that the conquering hero have an escort."

"Yes," said Nell, "you were wonderful, sir!"

Von Hoffman frowned a bit at Nell's effusiveness, but then nodded solemnly. "You are a great actor, Thompson. I salute you." The German extended his hand solemnly and Ranley shook it.

"That is good of you, Von Hoffman," returned his lordship.

"Yes, you were excellent," said Von Hoffman gravely. "I shall learn from you. I welcome you to our troupe." This remark caused Verity to direct an amused glance at the baron.

"That is kind of you, Von Hoffman," replied Ranley, "but I fear I cannot join the company. I only stepped in for Harold as a favor to Mumford. No, indeed, I shall soon be returning to London."

"That is a great pity," said Von Hoffman, who was actually very much relieved that the talented Mr. Thompson was not going to be a permanent addition to the troupe.

"It is a pity," said Verity. "But you doubtless have business in London which will cause you to return to town very soon."

"I have business here first, Mrs. Trelawney," replied Ranley. "When that is completed, I shall be pleased to return to town."

Verity and Ranley regarded each other for a moment, a fact noted by both Nell and Von Hoffman. "I do think we should be off for the Black Swan," said Verity. "Everyone will be wondering what happened to us."

The four of them proceeded to the inn where they were

roundly applauded by their fellow actors. Rising as they came in, Mumford raised his glass and proposed a toast. "To Mrs. Trelawney and Thompson. It is to them that we owe our great triumph!" This accolade brought three enthusiastic cheers from the other members of the troup.

Verity smiled graciously and thanked everyone as she took a seat among the actors. Ranley was happy to take a place beside her. There was an atmosphere of general merriment at the Black Swan. Mumford was especially jubilant for he had had a wonderful and extremely profitable night. It had been particularly gratifying to see the hostile audience completely won over by his old friend and the lovely Mrs. Trelawney.

Mumford did not doubt that if Ranley could be persuaded to stay with them even for a fortnight, they would do very well indeed. And even if the baron refused to perform again, Mumford knew that the talented Mrs. Trelawney was an enormously valuable asset. Once she had gained a reputation, audiences would come to see her no matter how lackluster the rest of the troupe might be.

Once flagons of ale were passed to the newcomers, Mumford continued to toast the great success of the company. The inn's servants then brought great trays of food to the table, much to the satisfaction of the famished company. Having already downed a good deal of the Black Swan's famous brew, Mumford and his fellow actors grew increasingly jolly as the night progressed.

As Verity sat beside the baron sipping her ale and eating roast beef and potatoes, she had a strange sense of unreality. Had she actually performed with Ranley on the stage? Was the baron actually sitting beside her there in an inn in Cornwall? It was like a dream. Whatever would her parents and friends think if they could see her at that moment?

She glanced over at the baron, happy that he was occupied in conversation with Miss Pettigrew. How dismayingly handsome he was and how utterly discomfitting it was to sit beside him. Verity could not help but remember the passionate kisses he had bestowed on her in the play.

Turning his attention from Miss Pettigrew, Ranley looked over at Verity. "So, Mrs. Trelawney, I expect you are enjoying your great success."

"I am enjoying myself, sir. I do hope you are as well."

Ranley grinned. "I don't think I have ever enjoyed myself so. I'll always remember this night, Lady Juliet."

This remark, said with such unexpected sincerity, seemed to take Verity aback. She was glad that the innkeeper chose that moment to approach and tap the baron on the shoulder. "This has come for you, Mr. Thompson." He handed Ranley a leather purse.

"What the devil!" cried his lordship, recognizing it as the one that had been stolen. "How did you get this?"

"A certain individual who will remain nameless brought it, sir. There is a note inside."

Ranley undid the drawstrings and opened the purse. Taking out a piece of paper, he read it to the company. "Dear Sir, I fancied the play you and the pretty lady was in. I reckon I never seen better. As I be so fond of the theater I regretted taking your purse so here it is. I kept some of the blunt for my troubles and the coat, hat, and watch, as I be too fond of them to give them up. Your obedient servant, Robert Tully."

This missive provoked much amusement among the company. The baron pronounced Bob Tully a villain, but joined in the laughter. "And now that I am a man of some resources once again," said Ranley. "I shall pay for this celebration. Oh, do not protest, my dear Mumford. I shall not be dissuaded." Mumford muttered a half-hearted protest before pronouncing "Thompson" as the finest man who ever lived. He then commanded the innkeeper to bring more food and ale.

After a time, Mumford called for everyone's attention. "My dear friends, I have had a wonderful idea. Indeed, it came to me just as I was finishing this delightful pork pie. In a few days' time we were to be bound for Devon, but

I have changed my mind. In view of our great success this evening, I think it more suitable that we go to London.''

This announcement caused great agitation among the actors. ''But where will we go, Father?'' said Harold.

''Our dear friend, Mr. Thompson, will assist us in finding a place. He is a man of influence. What say you, Thompson? You must know that Mrs. Trelawney will delight any London audience?''

''She would indeed,'' said Ranley, turning to smile at Verity. ''Yes, I think it a splendid idea for you to go to town. I guarantee that Mrs. Trelawney's appearance on stage will mean packed houses. I shall do everything I can to find a suitable place for you.''

Verity tried to appear unconcerned, but the idea of her appearing on stage in London was ridiculous. Of course, she could not return there. ''That is very good of you, Mr. Thompson,'' she said, ''but I am far too untried of an actress to go to London. I have so much to learn in the provinces. And I was so looking forward to going to Devon. I'm sure that everyone else was very eager to go there.'' Verity looked hopefully at her colleagues, but it was clear that London had much more appeal to them than the provinces.

Ranley smiled at Verity's discomfiture. ''Yes, London is the place for Mrs. Trelawney.''

''Yes, indeed,'' said Mumford. ''But we will speak more of this tomorrow. Do enjoy yourselves, my good friends.''

This admonition was readily heeded by everyone in attendance with the exception of Verity, who was none too pleased by the unexpected development. However, Von Hoffman began to speak to her and she was able to push the matter to the back of her mind.

The celebration continued unabated despite the fact that Harold Mumford fell noisily asleep at the table and Miss Pettigrew began to grow drowsy and slightly incoherent. There was a great deal of joking and banter, and as time went on, even the most ordinary remark was greeted as a great witticism.

As the hour grew late, several young gentlemen entered the inn. They were a loud and inebriated group who were boisterously slapping each other on the back and laughing in a raucous manner.

Ranley looked over at them, recognizing some of them as having been among the group of rowdy hecklers that had been in the hall. He frowned slightly, but he was in too good a mood to be much upset by their appearance.

Von Hoffman, encouraged by drink and the urgings of one of the other actors, broke into a Prussian drinking song. Ranley cast a tolerant smile at him, happy to find that the German was a better singer than he was an actor. The other actors joined in the singing despite the fact that no one seemed to know any of the songs or one bit of German.

It was a most memorable night, thought Ranley, looking at the happy faces of the company. Glancing over at Verity, who was lustily singing some nonsense syllables, he smiled. She was a very remarkable young lady, he found himself thinking. And damnably lovely sitting there in the candlelight, her face flushed and wisps of her raven hair falling across her forehead. How he wanted to take her into his arms. Yet, despite the increasingly muddled state of his mind, Ranley restrained himself.

"Mrs. Trelawney! May I be so bold as to remind you of our acquaintance?" A loud masculine voice caused both Verity and the baron to look behind them. There stood a well-dressed young gentleman and four of his friends.

Verity recognized Richard Baldwin, the sullen young man who had accompanied her to Cornwall. "Good evening, Mr. Baldwin," she said politely.

"You see, lads, she does remember me," said Richard grinning.

Verity eyed Richard with disapproval. She had not liked him. He had been sullen and unpleasant on the stagecoach, staring at her throughout the journey and scarcely saying a civil word.

"These gentlemen and myself wish to tell you, Mrs. Trelawney, that we considered your performance to be a marvel. Yes, a marvel, madam. We would be so very pleased if you would honor us by sharing a glass of wine at our table."

"That is very good of you, Mr. Baldwin, but I am otherwise engaged."

One of Richard's friends nudged him and he grinned again. "But I'm sure you could spare a moment, Mrs. Trelawney, for some gentlemen." He paused to regard the members of the company with a haughty look.

"I do thank you," said Verity with a frown, "but no."

Von Hoffman, irritated at the young man's demeanor, waved him away. "The lady answered you. She wishes you to be gone."

"And I shall thank you to keep quiet," returned Richard. "I was talking to Mrs. Trelawney, not some bloody foreigner."

Von Hoffman's face reddened and he started to rise from the table. "Now, now," cried Mumford, alarmed at Von Hoffman's enraged expression. "Do calm down, my dear Karl." He smiled amiably at Richard. "I think you young gentlemen might be off."

"And I think you might hold your tongue, my fat friend."

Mumford looked flustered at this rude retort. "Ill-mannered young puppy," he muttered.

The baron was trying hard to maintain his composure, but he had an almost overpowering urge to throttle Richard Baldwin. He was not a violent man, but there was something in the young man's bearing and expression that infuriated him. "Come along, Mrs. Trelawney. You belong in better company than this," said Richard.

"I see no better company," returned Verity, directing an icy stare at him.

Richard laughed. "Than this group of actors and vagabonds? You must be joking."

Ranley had by this time exhausted his patience. He rose from his chair and fixed a black look at the young man. "I suggest you take yourself and your friends away from here."

"Whom do you think you are addressing, actor?" said Richard indignantly.

"That is enough," said the baron, taking young Baldwin forcefully by the arm. "Now go!"

"Get your hands off of me," said Richard, pulling his arm away. To Ranley's surprise, the young man spun around and flailed out with his arm, hitting the baron squarely in the midsection.

Richard's friends shouted with glee and two of them jumped in to assist him pummel the baron. Fortunately for his lordship, the actors were upon his assailants in seconds and soon a melee had ensued. Young Baldwin's friends were joined by a group of rowdy youths eager for a fight of any kind. There was a dreadful commotion with screams from the women and shouts from the men.

Von Hoffman jumped into the fray with a zeal of a Teutonic warrior. He was a formidable fighter and soon had his adversaries bloodied and on the run. The ruckus did not last for very long, but when it was over, the public room of the Black Swan looked as if a long pitched battle had been fought there. Tables and chairs were overturned. Glasses and dishes of food were strewn everywhere.

The actors were pleased that they had successfully routed the youths, who had fled into the night. While the innkeeper stood wringing his hands and demanding that someone pay for damages, Verity hurried to Ranley, who was standing rather unsteadily and gingerly touching a bruise on his face.

"Are you alright, Ranley?" she said, taking his arm. "Do sit down."

He grinned. "I believe I am too old for brawling. I never was much good at it."

"It was quite disgraceful," said Verity severely, "although I warrant that Richard Baldwin was at fault."

"I am glad you ascertained that," said the baron wryly.

"Look, you are bleeding. Sit down, Mr. Thompson."
Ranley obediently sat down, pleased to suffer Verity's
ministrations. Sitting beside him, she took out her handkerchief to wipe the blood from a cut on his cheek. "I should
not help you at all after the way you encouraged Mr.
Mumford to go to London."

"That is where I think you belong. You cannot fault me
for doing what I think is best for you."

Seeing that he was sincere, Verity smiled. "Oh, I suppose
not." She dabbed again at his cheek. "It is not a very bad
cut."

"Perhaps you might kiss it to make it better," suggested
the baron. "The way my mother used to do."

"I am not your mother, sir," said Verity, suppressing a
smile.

"Yes, I am well aware of that," returned Ranley. Without
another word, he leaned forward and kissed her firmly on
the lips.

Although startled, Verity did not find this kiss at all
unwelcome. Aware only of him for the moment, she returned
the kiss with matching fervor. Then regaining her
composure, she managed to say reprovingly, "I did not think
your lips were injured, sir."

"No, thank God," said the baron, reaching his arms out
to her.

Eluding him, she rose to her feet. "You forget yourself,
sir."

"I suppose I do. Forgive me. It must be my injuries. Blows
to the head have addled me."

Ranley grinned and Verity could not help but laugh. "You
are incorrigible, sir. Well, it was an evening I shall not forget,
but it is time I went to bed."

"I would forget the evening even less if I might accompany
you," said the baron, directing an unmistakably suggestive
look at her.

"Mr. Thompson!" cried Verity. "You are addled
whatever the cause. Now, goodnight, sir!"

"Goodnight, sweet Juliet!"

Verity tried not to laugh as she turned away and hurried to find Nell.

22

Although the hour had been very late and she had been quite exhausted, Verity awakened early. Rising from bed, she put on her dressing gown and walked over to the window. There she stood for a time, peering out into the streets of Truro.

She found herself reflecting about the unforgettable events of the night before. Verity smiled, remembering her performance as Juliet and Ranley opposite her, acting as no one but he could do. A slight sigh escaped her lips and she turned away from the window. Whatever would she do about Ranley? She could not deny it any longer. She was in love with him. It was a dreadful complication.

Restless, Verity decided to take a walk. Not wishing to disturb Nell, she quietly dressed and slipped out of the bed-chamber. When she went downstairs and passed through the public room, she found a number of the inn's servants at work tidying the disarray that had been left the night before.

Verity shook her head as she thought of the brawl that had been the cause of the damage. It had been too ridiculous.

She smiled suddenly, thinking of Ranley. He had been the most ridiculous of all.

When she came outside, Verity noted the bright sunshine. She set off, walking briskly away from the inn. There was a narrow and evidently little used road that led away from the Black Swan into the countryside. She continued on, deep in thought and hardly aware of the fine weather and pleasant bucolic scenery. After a time, the road became little more than a path which led up a hill. Arriving at the top, Verity looked out upon a splendid view of the bay. She stood for a time, looking out at the brilliant blue green water.

"Good morning, fair Juliet!" A man's voice startled Verity who turned to see Ranley approaching.

"Ranley!" she said. "What are you doing here?"

"I have come to find you, my lady." He said, walking toward her. "Our excellent inkeeper said you had gone off. I was close on your heels. I will say you keep a damned fast pace, madam."

"I cannot imagine your rising so early, my lord. After last night's revelry, I thought you would sleep well into the afternoon."

The baron grinned. "If you think I was drunk last night, my dear lady, you are mistaken. I rose fresh as the proverbial daisy. And I could think of nothing but seeing you."

"Oh, do be serious, Ranley," said Verity severely.

"I am serious." He looked out at the bay. "It is lovely here. And lovelier still because sweet Juliet is at my side." Her warning look made him smile. "I wanted to talk with you. My carriage should arrive today. I want you to come back to London with me. You cannot stay here." Verity folded her arms in front of her, but said nothing. The baron continued. "You are a dashed fine actress. I have never seen better, and that is not idle flummery, but you cannot think this can continue."

"And why not?"

"Because you are Lady Verity de Lacy. You cannot run about the kingdom appearing as an actress. You must think of your family. I daresay your parents are beside themselves with worry. Lord Benbrook appeared very upset.''

"You saw my father?"

Ranley nodded. "I have seen him twice since your departure. He called on me."

"My father called on you?" said Verity, quite surprised.

The baron laughed. "The poor man thought I had eloped with you."

"What!" cried Verity in astonishment.

"There was a rumor going about town that you and I . . . Well, that you and I were more than acquaintances.''

"Oh, no!"

Ranley laughed again. "Your horror at the suggestion is hardly flattering.''

Verity could not help but smile. "It is only that the idea is so preposterous.''

"Yes," said his lordship. "Quite preposterous. Of course, people do enjoy believing such stories, outrageous though they may be. If you wish to stop these sort of rumors, you must come home.''

Verity frowned. "Even if I wished to do so, I don't see how I could. I will not marry Dorchester. Of course, I doubt he would still want me after my running off. And I do not wish to marry some other fool my father will throw at me.''

"I cannot see why you are so set against marriage."

Verity raised her eyebrows. "You, a bachelor, tell me this?"

"Well, I am not set against marriage. Indeed, I have of late been thinking it may have its advantages if one finds the proper lady. I myself have only just found her. I love you, Verity de Lacy.''

"Oh, Ranley, do not say that, not unless you truly mean it.''

"You are an infuriating vixen, Juliet," said the baron, reaching out to take her into his arms. "Of course I mean it. Why else would I have rushed out here after you like a damned idiot? If you cannot see that I am in love with you,

you are completely blind. You are the most stubborn, willful female I have ever known. I believe I knew the first time you fixed those beautiful blue eyes upon me that I had met my match.''

''Oh, Ranley,'' said Verity, looking up at him, ''I do love you with all my heart.'' Needing no further encouragement, the baron crushed Verity to him and covered her inviting mouth with his own.

Verity and Ranley stayed for a long time on the hill, and it was only reluctantly that they returned to the mundane realities of life. The most immediate impediment to Verity's happiness was the realization that she would have to tell Mumford that she was leaving the troupe. Although the baron assured her that his old friend would survive this cataclysm, Verity was quite distressed at abandoning a man who had been so kind to her and Nell.

It was therefore, the timeliest of *deus ex machinas* that upon their arrival back at the Black Swan, Verity and Ranley were greeted with the news that the difficult Miss Carrington had returned. Her new lover having proved quite unsatisfactory, the actress had soon regretted abandoning Mumford's troupe. She was back to beg Mumford to take her on again.

Although the theater director would have much preferred telling Miss Carrington that he had a far superior actress in her place, after hearing the startling news that Ranley was stealing his new leading lady from him, he had no choice but to welcome his former actress with open arms. It was a deep shock to Mumford and a crushing disappointment that he had to abandon his plans for a London triumph with the talented Mrs. Trelawney. Still, Mumford could not help but be pleased at his old friend's good fortune.

Everyone in the company, although likewise disappointed, offered their hearty congratulations upon hearing the news, proclaiming Mr. Thompson a very lucky man indeed. Nell was happiest of all. Not only was she glad to see that her mistress was going to marry a man she clearly loved, but the news meant that Nell could return once again to her career of lady's maid, a job she felt much better suited her than did the life of an actress. Indeed, Nell was only too eager to leave the life she had previously thought would be so exciting.

As Ranley had predicted, his carriage arrived shortly after they had returned to the inn. The baron was adamant about leaving as soon as possible, telling Verity that he did not dare give her time to change her mind. Therefore, the following day, Ranley, Verity, and Nell found themselves back on the road to London.

When they finally arrived in town, it was with some trepidation that Verity entered Benbrook House. Accompanied by Ranley and Nell, she asked the startled and happy butler if her parents were home.

"Indeed so, my lady," said Weeks, smiling broadly at seeing that his young mistress had returned. "They are in the drawing room."

"We shall go directly in," said Verity, taking Ranley's arm. She looked up at him. "I do hope Papa does not toss us from the doorstep."

"My dear Verity, I share that sentiment quite strongly," returned the baron with a smile.

Verity's misgivings were quite unfounded for upon seeing her beloved daughter reappearing in the drawing room, the countess fell upon Verity's neck with sobs. "You are back!"

"Oh, Mama," said Verity, "I am so sorry!"

The earl noted Ranley's presence with suspicion. "So you are with my daughter, Ranley?"

"Yes, indeed, Lord Benbrook."

"Oh, Papa," said Verity once she had extricated herself from her mother's embrace. "Can you ever forgive me?"

Benbrook tried to appear gruff. "Oh, dammit," he said finally. "I suppose I shall. I always do."

A delighted Verity rushed to hug her father. "Dear Papa!"

Once the tearful reunion had been accomplished, the countess commanded everyone to be seated. "Where have you been? Where did you go?"

"Oh, I have had a great adventure. I know you will be very angry."

The earl frowned first at Verity and then Ranley. "I daresay I shall be," he said. "You have been gone over three weeks. You sent us letters, but never told us where you were or how you were living."

"Oh, Papa. I do not want you to have a fit of apoplexy. Do stay calm."

"I'll not stay calm if you do not proceed to tell me what you were doing. I want the truth."

Verity nodded. "Nell and I went to Cornwall. I had some money from the play I sold."

"The play you sold!" cried Lady Benbrook. "Whatever can you mean, Verity?"

"*Valiant Lady,*" interjected Ranley. "Everyone thinks it was my play, but Lady Verity wrote it. It is rather a long story."

"It is an excellent play," said the countess. "How very clever of you, Verity."

"Thank you, Mama. I pray you allow me to continue. We went to Cornwall, Nell and I, on the stagecoach. I intended to live for a time there and write another play. But then we met Mr. Mumford and he offered me a position in his theater troupe."

"Oh dear," cried Lady Benbrook, placing a hand upon her chest."

"My daughter a common actress!" cried Benbrook.

"She was rather a most uncommon actress," said Ranley. "She was splendid."

"That does not surprise me," said the countess, "but Verity! An actress! How could you?"

"And what do you have to do with all this, Ranley?" demanded the earl.

"I had a letter from my old friend Mumford—he is the

director of the theater troupe—and I suspected the new actress he described might be Lady Verity. Since I could not be sure, I decided to go to Cornwall myself.''

"That was very good of you, Lord Ranley," said the countess.

"Was it?" said the earl sourly. "And then?"

"And then," said Verity, "Ranley convinced me to come back to London to be married."

"He did?" said the earl. He looked at the baron. "Then I am in your debt, sir. But I fear, Verity, that you are too late. Dorchester will not have you. Under the circumstances I could not argue with him. The engagement is broken off."

"Oh, that is a pity," said Verity with a smile. "But I do have another offer." She directed a mischievous look at Ranley. "He is not so grand as Dorchester, of course, but he is misguided enough to wish to be my husband. Mama and Papa, Ranley has asked me to marry him."

"Ranley?" said the earl. "Why, I must consider this."

"I know you have reason to be less than happy at the prospect of me for a son-in-law, Lord Benbrook," said Ranley, "but I do have a respectable income. And I do love your daughter. I shall devote myself to her happiness."

"And I do love him," said Verity.

"I don't know," said Benbrook uncertainly. "It is not that I dislike you, Ranley, but it is this business of your once having been an actor."

"Oh, do not be a stick, my dear," said the countess. "That was some time ago. I think our daughter could do far worse."

Although the earl was not at that moment convinced of that, he finally nodded. "You are a brave man," said Benbrook, reaching out to shake Ranley's hand. Verity laughed and hugged her father.

When they were finally able to have a few moments alone in the garden of Benbook House, Verity took Ranley's arm. "I can scarcely believe it. We have my parents' blessing."

The baron smiled. "I suspect your father has his doubts."

"Well, he will love you. They both will. You are quite lovable."

"Am I?" said Ranley. "I daresay, you did not always think so. You for some time seemed to dislike me."

Verity smiled up at him. "That, my lord, is only because I am a very good actress." The baron laughed and, taking his smiling lady into his arms, he kissed her jubilantly.